GLITCH

By Briana Michaels

COPYRIGHT

All names, characters and events in this publication are fictitious and any resemblance to actual places, events, or real persons, living or dead, is entirely coincidental.

All rights reserved. No part of this publication may be reproduced, stored, or transmitted, in any form or by any means, without the prior permission, in writing, of the author.

www.BrianaMichaels.com

COPYRIGHT © 2022 Briana Michaels

DEDICATION

For all the dirty minded, filthy mouthed, smut loving readers out there:
May you always come so hard, your mind and body both GLITCH.

CHAPTER 1

Glitch

"Touch yourself for me." I lean in and lick my lips before sucking in a harsh breath through my clenched teeth. "Just like that. Be a good little slut and rub your clit. That's it. Mmm. Just like that. Go faster. Harder. Ffffuck. That's my dirty girl. Keep going." I inhale sharply. "Now *stop*." My heart's racing a mile a minute. "Start again. Slowly, slowly. Mmm. You are so beautiful like this. All worked up and dripping for me." I count down from ten in my head. *Ten, nine, eight, seven...* When I reach one, "Stop."

My cell lights up, the screen showing sixteen notifications. Those texts can wait.

"Show me how wet you are for my cock." I wait a few beats before adding, "Look at you. So perfect and swollen. Ah, ah, ah, I didn't say you could touch yourself again." My deep, throaty chuckle rumbles in my chest. "Give me your hand. I want to know what you taste like. Mmm. That's good. But we can make it better. Fuck yourself with two fingers for me." I lean back, quietly taking a sip of water and make sure to swallow nice and loud. "God, you get me so hard." *Five, four, three, two…* "Stop."

I exhale a ragged breath. "Look at you. So needy and desperate to come. Do you ache? Do you want to be *fucked*?" I lick my lips. "If you want to come so badly, let me hear you beg for it." I grumble another deep laugh. "I like it when you beg. I like it more when you spread your legs like that so I can see everything that's mine. Damn, that's a pretty pussy." I growl deep like a primal beast. "I'm not finished having fun with you yet. Stroke your clit until I tell you to stop." I count down from three this time. "Stop."

Leaning forward, my lips nearly brush against the microphone. "Such a good girl. Do it again and don't stop until you cream." I suck in yet another harsh breath. Pant a little.

My phone lights up again, distracting me. Damnit.

Hitting a button to stop recording, I snag my cell and answer. "What's up?"

"We're just waiting on you, man."

What time is it? *Shit*. "Be right there."

I hang up and tuck the cell into my back pocket.

Leaving the closet that's kitted out with my audio recording equipment, I saunter down the hall. I live in a three-bedroom townhouse, alone, so I turned one of the extra bedrooms into a gaming room. Three large screens line my desk.

Starting my computer, I watch the sides glow in neon colors as it boots up. My ass hits the chair and I tip it back, logging into Discord before hopping into the lobby of our newest game.

"Sorry about that." I type into the chat sidebar. I don't like talking into my microphone, especially when Ara is online with us.

"No problem, man. We've got all the time in the world for you to get your dick out of your hand."

I'm going to punch Trey next time I see him. For now, I type back, "It takes *two* hands to hold my dick."

"Ugh, stop talking about your swizzle sticks!" This coming from Ara. "Let's kick some zombie ass!"

"Well, someone woke up and chose violence today," Trey laughs.

I glance over at my Discord channel and see Ara's already left me a message.

Ara666: *Hot date?*

Glitch: *Nah, just caught up in work stuff.*

Sometimes when I'm recording a script, I lose track of time. Especially when Ara's the one I'm fantasizing about.

Glitch: *How's it going?*

I don't care about Trey or Carson waiting. They can play without me. But I don't like the fact that I might have wasted Ara's time. She hasn't been on in a while and never plays long when she is. Her boyfriend takes up a lot of her time.

Lucky fucker.

If she belonged to me, I'd be even worse. She wouldn't have a spare minute to breathe unless it's to scream my name while I fuck her, spoil her, and worship her.

Okay, wow. I need to chill.

Ara666: *Okay. Been busy. I'm glad I have a night off to play with you guys. I've missed hanging out.*

Ara and I have a weird relationship. We skate around the personal stuff, which was fine for a while. But I've been dying to take the plunge and ask more questions for months. I want to know everything about this woman. So far, even with the chat I keep open between us, she doesn't really divulge much. Maybe she likes to keep this part of her life drama free.

Glitch: *How's the boyfriend?*

His name's Jason, but I call him Cocksucker in my head all the time. Ara's usually busy with him, which is one of the reasons she doesn't get to play with us often.

Ara666: *Broke up a few weeks ago.*

If she didn't already have all my attention, she does now. I pull my headphones off and lean forward to stare at those six perfect words. *Broke up a few weeks ago*. They broke up *weeks* ago? My heart pounds in my ears.

Glitch: *Sad or happy? Do I need to get out champagne or a shovel?*

Ara doesn't answer, and it takes me a hot minute to realize it's because they've started the game without me. I put my headphones back on and turn up the volume.

"Ara!" chirps Carson in a whiney voice.

"Suck it, Carson," she shoots back.

God damn. Her voice never fails to make me insta-hard. It drips into my brain and pumps hella hot blood straight to my cock. She's the only reason I have my volume so loud. If I could filter her voice, and only hers, I'd mute the rest of the world.

My cock twitches when she asks, "Why do I always have to carry your sorry asses?"

Carson laughs like a hyena and says something obnoxious back. I can't stand the pitch of his voice, or how he talks so much shit. He's a hundred times worse whenever Ara plays with us. It drives me insane.

Trey introduced us to Ara as "one of the guys" when she first started playing with us. He's not wrong. That woman can sling insults better than most and she never gets her feelings hurt when anyone trash talks. If anything, Carson has probably spent a few nights licking his wounds after she's handed him his ass.

Ara is a unicorn. The perfect trifecta of a dirty mouth, ballsy attitude, and a beautiful laugh.

I've never met her face to face. Never asked what she looks like or what she does for a living beyond "makes art". And as far as I know, she's never asked Trey about me either. That's fine. Distance is good. It allows me to keep the masterpiece I've painted of her in my mind going without interference.

And I'm cool with keeping the Discord channel up for as long as she wants. Sometimes it makes me feel like a dog waiting for a little attention, but that's on me. She hasn't led me on or done anything to spur this obsession I have for her.

I did this to myself.

Trey respawns and starts shooting again. "You've been MIA, girl."

Trey is a graphic designer. I've got my audio gig at night and run a gaming shop during the day. Carson is a photographer with zero people skills who occasionally works with Trey. Trey and I went to college together and he's the one who has a connection to each of us and is usually the one to bring up touchy subjects first. For once, I'm grateful he has, because I'd like to know where she's been too. It's sucked playing without her.

"Aww, did you guys miss me?"

Carson chuckles. "I'm sure *someone* here has."

I want to throat-punch him.

Before I type or utter a word, Trey says, "We were worried. Thought you might have moved on to bigger and better."

Ara's right on it. "Bigger assholes than you exist?"

"Oh! Shots fired!" Carson laughs.

I wait for Ara to say that her and Jason have broken up. I secretly like that maybe I'm the only one who knows that much. Some part of me relishes that maybe she confided only in me.

Ara doesn't say anything more. In fact, she's radio silent. I look over to see she's not online and turn to Discord.

Glitch: *You good?*

She doesn't answer. An uneasy tightness grips my chest.

Glitch: *Are you okay?*

Ara666: *My computer is being a dicktwat.*

Ara666: *I'm rebooting.*

She pops back up soon after. "Sorrrrryyyy! My computer is being stupid, so I moved to my laptop and it's so slow."

"What's wrong with your computer?" Trey asks. *Nosey fucker*.

"I don't know. It hates me."

Trey groans. "You kicked it, didn't you?"

I can't hold in my laugh. It's deep and grumbly, even as I try to keep it quiet.

"Dayem, Glitch," Ara says, and I can hear her smile. "You've got a serious set of pipes."

"Glitch can set off alarms and start avalanches with his register."

I hate Carson. Have I said that already? Before I get twitchy, I redirect them. "Alright, alright, get back to the game, fuckers."

Look, I know some people have a thing for voices—it's how I make decent cash with my side hustle—but I hate when it becomes a joke. Even if it's a harmless one. Yeah, yeah, go ahead and eye roll me, but my voice sounds like I've swallowed a box of rocks mixed with glass shards. It might be great now, but it sure as shit wasn't when I was growing up.

As a freshman whose voice dropped before most of his peers, I got singled out a lot.

Want to watch a guy turn into a bully? Threaten his testosterone level.

Students at my school made such a big deal about my voice that by the time I was fifteen, no one called me by name anymore. They called me Deep Throat. I was so mortified, I didn't have the sense to say anything back. I shut down and didn't socialize anymore.

Back then, I was awkward and spindly and shy on my bravest day. Once my vocal cords became a source of entertainment and a way to target and treat me like shit, I clammed up and didn't speak at all. Not to my classmates. Not to my teachers. And not to my grief counselor when my parents passed away.

I spent my high school life with guys hating me, and girls afraid of me. I didn't find my groove until college, and it's still shaky sometimes.

"I'll probably have to take my computer somewhere to get it fixed, but I'm going to try a couple more things on my own first," Ara says, making my heart run off with my balls. I should offer to fix it for her. I want to. But…

"Come on Ara, pick up your lady dick and quit lagging."

"If I pick up my lady dick, will you stop tripping over it? Or should I smack you in the face with it to get you to actually *hit* a target, asshole?"

"She's not wrong, Carson." Trey laughs. "You suck at this game."

I listen while they go on and on, slinging insults and racking up points. I always carry the team when I'm on, so while they run around and do what they can, I do my thing.

"Suck my *dick*!" Ara squeals as she wipes out a bunch of zombies at once. Then she assassinates both Trey and Carson, because this is a one-player-takes all game.

Everyone starts shooting off at the mouth, screaming and calling her all kinds of names.

Everyone but me.

I want to tear them limb-from-limb for talking shit to her. That includes my best friend, Trey. My hands grip the controller so hard, the case cracks. But it's her laugh that stops me from following through with the threats racing around in my mind. I loosen my grip on the controller. My heart still races as I ease back in my chair, but I'm no longer seeing red.

If she's okay with them talking trash, then I'll try my best to suck it up too. She's a grown ass woman. If she didn't like it, she'd shut them up herself. Or leave the game.

"When are you going to marry me, Arabella?" Trey's register drops when he asks. He *always* asks her this. It always pisses me off.

"I'd rather suck on a dead pig's foot than be your wife."

Fuck. What a woman.

We play until there's one of us left alive. It's her. Usually is. Without a word, we start another game. This goes on for another hour — the bantering, me getting mad; me staying quiet. Ara winning. Another game starts up and I keep my eyes on **Ara666**. Even her name on the side of the screen is pretty.

Jesus, I've got it bad.

My cell vibrates my ass cheek, and I reach into my back pocket to snag it. *Shit*. Knocking my headphones off, I answer my phone and pinch it between my ear and shoulder so I can keep playing. "Hey little dude. What's up?"

"Can you play Minecraft with me?"
"Right now?"
"Yes."

"Yeah, hang on." Listen, when my nine-year-old nephew asks me to play a game, I play. Doesn't matter that I can't stand the games he's into. I will jump in and play until his mother tells him he has to shut down his console and go to bed. "Can you give me five minutes?"

"Yeah."

"Thanks, Beetle."

"Don't hang up with me," he says in a hurry.

Uh oh. When he says shit like that it means he's having a bad day and is clingy. "Not going anywhere." I finish up the game in silence and sign off, because dropping out mid-game is a dick move and I wouldn't do that to Ara. The others? Yes. I'd drop them in a heartbeat, but not her.

"Okay, I'm all yours." I move to play Minecraft in the living room. Listen, building a world with a nine-year old takes forever. The least I can do for myself is get comfortable while I make castles and kill ender dragons. "How was your day?"

Non-Parent Parent Tip: Some kids have trouble sharing their feelings. Give them a controller and a screen, and they'll usually open up. I've seen it a million times over the years. Adults are no different. It's easier to vent when you aren't staring someone in the face so they can see your emotions.

And getting kids to open up is important.

Trust me, I know.

Refusing to let my nephew suffer any of the trauma I dealt with growing up, I vowed the day my sister told me she was pregnant that I'd never let him feel alone.

"I got an infraction at school."

"For what?"

"Hitting a kid."

"Mmmph." I drop it for now because I need to tread carefully about subjects like this. I'll get to the bottom of it, because he shouldn't be fighting, period. But I also know my nephew wouldn't do something like that without good reason. "Which realm are we going into?"

"SeaMonster Superdemon."

That's the newest one we've made with two kids from his school who trash talk worse than Carson. I click on it and wait for instructions. Beetle usually has a plan on what he wants to build next. When he doesn't say anything, I pipe up with, "Waiting on you, dude."

Silence.

"Beetle?" I look at my phone and see we've been disconnected. Shit. I call back and he picks up on the fourth ring.

"Dude, the f—" *Don't cuss.* "You okay?" I can hear him breathing into the phone. These short, angry spurts of air funnel into my ears and I go on high alert. "Beetle, what's wrong?"

"THEY STOLE OUR STUUUUUFFFF!"

It takes me a few seconds to realize he's not talking about being robbed in real life but in the game. *Awww shit*. I look at our world, where our towers use to be, the treasure chests hidden underground.

"They took *everything*, Uncle Glitch!"

Yes. They. Did.

I want to tell him it's fine. That it's just a game. That it doesn't really matter because we can make a new world. But that's not true. It's not just a game, it's his outlet. It matters to him. He's spent all his allotted screen time building this world with his brilliant little mind, and I refuse to downplay this catastrophe.

Those two classmates he invited to play and create in his world have destroyed it instead.

"Beetle!" I hear my sister Erin yell in the background. She must have thought he was hurt the way she panicked. I don't blame her. He's spitting mad and acting out, which is something they're working on. "What's wrong?"

"They stole everything from my fucking world!" he screams at her.

Oh shit. Oh shit, oh shit, oh shit.

My sister grabs the cell from him, and I cringe when she says, "Glitch, you better not be the one to have taught him that word."

I'm not. But my sister will never admit she has a foul mouth and no filter. Beetle didn't get the f-bomb from me, that's a promise, but he might have picked it up at home, or at school. "Wasn't me."

Beetle yells angrily in the background.

"Damnit," Erin sighs. "I'll call you back."

"Hey, don't yell at him, okay? He's been riding the struggle bus a lot lately." Worst. Thing. I. Could. Have. Said.

Erin goes dead quiet.

"Shit, Erin. I'm sorry I—"

"Don't talk to me like you know my son better than me, Glitch." She hangs up on me and I stare at the TV screen. The pixelated image that once was a sprawling, exciting world my nephew created out of brilliance and patience was destroyed.

Kids are assholes. And now my sister thinks I'm an asshole too. Damnit.

My cell dings. Bracing for a nasty text from Erin, I swallow the lump in my throat and look down.

Trey: *Sorry man. It had to be done.*

What the—

Another text comes through just as I'm typing a response back. It's from an unknown number and when I click on it, my heart stops.

Unknown: *Hey Glitch, it's Ara. Trey gave me your number and said you agreed to look at my computer. Thanks so much for this. I'll do anything to get this baby up and running again. When and where can we meet?*

I read it three times.

I can't breathe.

Of course, I'll look at her computer. I was going to offer on our Discord channel privately—because I hate when other people get all in my business—and she's not paying me a dime for anything I do for her.

Still, I'm pissed at Trey. He's trying to shove us together when I'd rather do this my own way.

Trey: *You can thank me later.*

He thinks he's done me a favor. He has no idea Ara and I chat privately on Discord sometimes, but really, what has that gotten us? Nowhere in months. We're too cautious, too generic, and safe. Too filtered and buffered. And she's been too taken by someone else.

Until now.

I keep opening her text to send an answer and closing it before I do.

Open. Close. Open. Close.

This is why my sister started calling me Glitch when I was a kid. If I'm not in control, my wires cross and brain fritzes. I lose all chill. Get stupid really fucking fast. Damn Trey for this.

Popping open the text again, I'm so mad my thumbs fly across the screen.

Glitch: *I'm going to wrap my hands around your throat and squeeze until you see God.*

I smash the send button, realizing my mistake too late. FUCK!

I sent the message to Ara, not Trey.

CHAPTER 2

Ara

I was nervous about texting Glitch. Stupid, right? We chat on Discord sometimes, but I don't know. Having his cell feels… different. More intimate? I don't know why it feels that way.

Okay. Yes, I do. But I'm not about to admit that I've fallen for a guy I barely know, who I've never seen, and who has basic conversations with me online. It's embarrassing. I haven't said a word about it to Trey, and I sure as shit would never say anything to Carson, but Glitch has been a constant tip-toe area for months.

Coming to him with a broken computer is not how I thought we'd finally meet. I don't like asking for help. I also don't like it when things are fucked up. It makes me feel messy and out of control. As an artist, I don't mind mess on canvas. Hell, I don't mind chaos on canvas either. But that's my mental space. My control. I tell the paint where to go. When shit breaks around me and I can't fix it? That's next level anxiety.

I stress a lot. When I'm painting, I'm in a calm-zone, but the instant I step back, self-doubt and imposter syndrome creep in. Gaming is my stress reliever. With everything I've had going on lately, I've barely been online.

And the only other stress reliever I have comes with a rechargeable battery.

I suck at being social. I hate big crowds. I'm an awkward turtle who is obsessed with anime, gaming, and art. God bless Trey for including me on these nights. When he called to say Glitch would work on my computer, relief made me twenty pounds lighter. I'm desperate.

And I'm pissed.

Yes, my computer was kicked. And ever since, it's gotten worse and worse when I use it.

Walking away from frustration—*my broke ass computer*—I leave my phone on the kitchen table and head into my bedroom.

While other women my age are clubbing on this fine Friday night, I'm in my bed with noise canceling headphones and a battery boyfriend by my side. Look, I'd love to have a hot guy in here with me, but that requires more effort than I'm willing to give. Dating sites suck, as my last three boyfriends have proven. Bars and clubs are noisy and overpriced and fun for a half a minute. I'm not good at socializing and have no intention of throwing my insecure ass out there to get rejected again.

I wish I could feel pathetic, but I don't. I'm sick of being burned. Sick of being told I'm not good enough, not skinny enough, not fun enough. I tell that to myself daily. I don't need it reinforced by another shitty boyfriend.

Glitch not included.

I can't imagine what he'd be like as a boyfriend. I can't even imagine would he *looks* like. But his online personality—God, I hope it's real—is wonderful. He's encouraging and funny. He makes me feel… *safe*. Just having his Discord channel open makes me feel like I have a place to go if I need it. Which is stuuuuupiiiiddd. I know, I know. But have you ever felt a connection with someone and can't explain how that could be possible? That's Glitch for me.

And I love his voice. It's so fucking deep, it gives me goosebumps every time he says something, which isn't nearly often enough. His laugh tonight made me wet. I'm so glad I live alone. I'd die if someone caught the wet spot I have in my leggings.

Laying back on my pillows, I close my eyes and picture what a night with Glitch would be like. I'm a creative woman, and I've spent months painting visions of this man in my head. We talk a lot in my fantasies. And his mouth is as dirty as my mind…

> *"Heyyy, Kitty."*
> My smile nearly splits my face. *Meow.*
> *"Did you miss me?"*
> *Yes.*
> *"I couldn't get you off my mind."*

Same.
"Did you wear this outfit all day?"
Yes.
"Turn around. Let me see you."

I imagine spinning in a slow, sensual circle where I sway my hips and give him a nice show of every curve I possess. They all belong to him…

"Fuck, you're stunning. Look how hard you make me." He sucks in air through his teeth. Grunts. "I want to gouge out the eyes of every man who looked at you today."

I bite my lip again. Glitch says the sweetest things.

"This," he growls, all primal and deep in my ears, "is mine."

My cheeks heat.

"Take off your clothes. I want to see what I own."

I shimmy out of my leggings and almost knock the kitty-eared headset off when I pull my shirt over my head. With my eyes closed and imagination in overdrive, it almost feels like this could be a little bit real. I envision Glitch with tats down his arms, big hands and dark hair, but I never see his face. I just can't picture it, ever.

"Lay back and spread your legs for me, Kitty."

I do as he says. I pretend he calls me Kitty only because of one conversation we had when I told him I got a new pair of headphones that had cat ears. I love these things and wanted to geek out about them to someone. Glitch was my someone. Next time we were online, he typed, "Hey Kitty, how was your day?" and I nearly squealed. He never called me Kitty again, but that's okay. He calls me that all the time in my fantasies.

"Look at you," I pretend he purrs in my ears. *"So wet already. Did you think about me today, Kitty?"*

I think about you all the time.

"Did you think about my cock? Your body was built just for me to play with and pleasure."

Bzzzzzzz. I grip my toy like a weapon for big-time clitoral damage.

"Show me where you want it."

I spread my legs and set my toy right where it needs to be. With my other hand, I graze my fingertips over my tits and pinch my nipple.

"So needy," he grumbles, and I imagine his register dips even lower. My body is already coiling. Tightening.

"I can't get you out of my head, Ara. I need to taste you. Fuck, I need to — " His words cut off, replaced with a deep, throaty primal sound that makes my toes curl. His breaths punch out, like he's having trouble controlling his urges around me. I imagine he exhales a ragged breath and says, *"Open your mouth, Kitty. Let me feed you my cock."*

In my head, I obey. And when I imagine him groaning, as if I feel so good to him he can't contain his noises, I feel a hot ribbon coil tighter inside myself.

To be the one who makes a sexy man break. To feel so unbelievably good, he unravels at the touch of my lips.

Real or fake, it does things to me.

I play with my clit, imagining I'm sucking him off.

He grunts and shoves deeper down my throat. "I'm gonna come."

Me too.

I'm too far gone in sensations to hold up my imagination. My head gets a little fuzzy. "Glitch." I shove two fingers inside my pussy and turn up the vibration on my toy.

"Such a needy girl."

I imagine his breaths pick up and start to match mine. Every cell in my body sets on fire and the orgasm I have makes me explode. My pussy clenches. My clit's swollen. I'm dripping between my legs by the time I'm done.

Laying on my back, I struggle to regain focus. My cheeks tingle. I'm limp and thirsty.

With my ears still ringing, I meander into the kitchen for a glass of water. Leaning on the counter, I sigh with a stupid smile on my face. Glitch is the best lover I've never had.

Too tired to sketch tonight, and too wired to sleep, I'm not sure what else to do. Maybe hop online again and see if the guys are still up and playing? Trey doesn't have a life. He's probably still up.

Hmmm.

I go over to my computer and boot it up. The fans run, the lights brighten and then…

Shutdown.

Damnit.

I hate using my laptop, so I refuse to even consider it again. At least Glitch is willing to look at my computer. I hope he can fix it. Speaking of—

I snatch my cell and see he's sent a reply.

Glitch: *I'm going to wrap my hands around your throat and squeeze until you see God.*

Wow. I… I'm not even sure what to say to that. Maybe this is a joke? Fuck knows Carson and Trey are always talking shit. Blame it my post-orgasmic haze, but his reply about choking me out throws a curve ball to my imagination. One I'll happily catch and lob right back.

You want to play, Glitch? Let's play.

Biting my lip, I punch in my response.

CHAPTER 3

Glitch

I glare at my phone so hard it's a miracle it hasn't incinerated in my hand.

Ara: *Sounds fun. Does this service cost extra?*

I accidentally sent her a text about strangulation, and she sends me this back?

I'm in so much trouble.

The smile on my face gets ten kinds of wicked. I should have known she wouldn't get offended. As bad as I want to respond with something dirty, I don't. I'm already in my head too much with this woman. Have been since game one. In fact, every skit I've written for the past six months has been with her in mind. I've never let anyone hear them, but I enjoy the Kitty Series I've started on nights when I can't get Ara out of my fucking head.

I clutch my phone, imagining what it would be like to collar her throat with my hand. Make her purr.

My dick is so hard it hurts.

Stay focused, asshole. I need to respond with something non-dirty. Because if I'm going to use my words, I'll say them with my filthy fucking mouth, not a text.

Glitch: *I have a shop in Huntington called the Computer Cave. Is that too far for you?*

Shit, I don't even know where she lives. Trey's a couple hours away from me, does she live by him? Or maybe she lives in an entirely different state. No, wait. Trey wouldn't have set this up unless it was doable.

Ara: *I drive by that place all the time!*

My heart thuds in my throat. She must live close to me then. Holy shit, what are the chances?

Glitch: *You can drop it off anytime and put my name on the ticket.*

I have a lot of customers roll through my store daily, and this might make me sound like a possessive caveman, but I'm not going to tolerate anyone else touching her things. It's me or no one. If my name goes on the ticket, no one will even think about touching it.

I see the little dots appear and hold my breath, awaiting her answer.

Ara: *I'll do that. Thanks. Good night.*

I'm left deflated. Not sure what I thought was going to happen there, but my cock tents my gym shorts and it's pouting. I might have missed an opportunity with this exchange, but I'm not the kind of guy who communicates through text well. I fucking hate it. Tones are misconstrued, meanings are taken wrong, and winky faces are annoying.

She'll drop off her computer at some point and we'll go from there. Maybe I'll ask her out for coffee. If she's freshly broken up with her boyfriend, does that mean she's rebounding? I feel sick thinking someone else might comfort her instead of me. Rebound or not, I'll take my chances. It's been torture playing games without her. Shit. It's been torture playing games *with* her. I'm making my fucking move when I see her at the shop.

But I still want to strangle Trey for this set up.

I'd have worked the nerve up to make a move on her eventually, without his help.

Maybe.

Aww, who am I kidding? I've spent months obsessing over her and I still haven't tried to take things beyond the generic, safe conversations we have on Discord. I'm being a coward, which isn't like me at all.

Hey, I'm great once the ice breaks. I'm shit at breaking it first. Trey was always better at that than me. I get too in my head because no matter who it is—the bartender, the waitress, the eighty-five-year-old librarian, my nephew's teacher, shit, even my Uber eats delivery driver—people can't not make a face or have some reaction to my voice when I speak. It makes me uncomfortable when they turn red or gawk or have something to say about it—like ask if I do porn (yes, I've been asked that a lot) or sometimes a woman will ask me to say something specific, which is awkward as fuck when you're just trying to order a coffee and donut. Flirtations get weird. And making the first move has never been my strong suit.

Taking the reins afterwards is.

In fact, I've had women hand me control and get on their knees without my asking. Which means my voice is as much a weapon as it is an incentive.

One I rarely use.

Feeling inspired, I decide to make another recording. Usually, I type out a skit and tweak it until it's up to my standards, but tonight I don't have the patience for it. Heading into my closet/recording booth, I sit down and prime a new track. Rubbing my hands together, I realize I'm a little juiced about this. Smashing the record button, I close my eyes and drop into a scene.

"Heyyyy, Kitty." I wet my lips and smile. "Why don't you crawl over here? That's it. Nice and slow."

I imagine Ara dropping to her hands and knees and crawl to me like a cat. Her tits spill out of a pink, lace bra and jiggle just enough to make my balls ache.

"Did you miss this cock?" My heart beats faster. "Open your mouth so I can give you a gift." I suck in air through my clenched teeth.

"Wider." I salivate, thinking of Ara tipping her head back, opening a pair of beautiful lips like a good girl, and waiting anxiously for my present. "Stick your tongue out. More. MORE." I spit close to the mic and catch it in my palm. "Good girl. Now lick the base of my cock."

Still standing, I drop my pants, and the mic is close enough to the edge of my table that it catches the sound of my slick-with-spit palm stroking my dick. I lean over and suck in another breath. Let out a growl. "Ffffuuuuccckkk, you feel good when you lick me like that. Now get up. Ah-ah-ah…" I wag my finger. "What happens when you take more than I tell you? That's right. You don't want to be spanked already, do you? I thought you were my good girl." I groan, my cock heavy and hot in my hand. "Show me what a good girl does."

At this point, I imagine Ara sucking me down to the base. Gagging on me. Pulling my balls and sucking one into her mouth and rolling her tongue over it. "That's right, Kitty." I stroke myself harder, faster. "You want this cream, don't you? Yeahhhh, you do. Suck me harder and let me give it to you."

My balls tighten. Heat blooms across my back, my thighs lock. With a low, deep rumble, I come all over my desk, the base of the mic, and even manage to hit the fucking keyboard. It feels too good to care.

"That's my Kitty. Lick it clean. You waste a drop, then we're going to have to do this all over again." Because I can come five times without needing a break.

I tap the record button again to stop it and clean up. The scene was short, sweet, and just enough to almost take the edge off.

I can't wait to finally meet the muse who makes my dick ache.

CHAPTER 4

Ara

I didn't get to the shop Glitch told me about until Thursday. I felt terrible about it at first, but really, it's not like I made an appointment, and he didn't say I had to come immediately. I've been trying my best to fix the problem myself so I wouldn't have to go at all. He'll know what happened the second he sees it, and I don't want to explain myself. But I also don't want to lie to him. It feels wrong to start off with a fib. Even if this thing between us goes nowhere, I just don't think I can do it.

Relax. He's fixing your computer, not your life.

I really need to chill. It's just a drop off. Nothing more.

But I want more.

Nope. I *think* I want more.

Really, I don't know what the fuck I'm doing lately. My life's a mess. I can't get my muse to come out of hiding, so everything I've been painting is trash, and I'm in desperate need to get laid. And… okay, this is the real truth… I dumped my whacko boyfriend, who keeps showing up at odd times of the day and night. I never know when he's going to bang on my door drunk, or call me begging to take him back, or be waiting at my favorite coffee shop with a muffin for me. It's annoying and exhausting. And scary.

Pulling into the parking lot, I'm a little surprised I haven't been to the Computer Cave before. I've driven past it a bunch of times, but never thought to go in. It's in a strip mall, on the busy side of town. Anime and game posters are displayed in the big windows. The green neon OPEN sign glows brightly beneath an electric blue *Computer Cave* sign.

I grab my computer and find myself hesitating at the door. I'm going to meet Glitch. This is it. The guy I've been low-key swooning over for months is right on the other side of this door. Is he tall? Bulky? Inked?

My heart flutters in my chest.

Wow. That I'm this excited to meet this guy in person proves I really need to socialize more often. He's only fixing my computer, not fucking me.

Okay. Whoa. Where'd that thought come from?

Simmer down, hot sauce. You're here for your computer, not your libido.

The door opens. "Coming in?"

I stand there until my cheeks grow hot. "Y-yeah. Sorry." I scoot past the man and head inside, clutching my heavy computer to my chest like I'm two seconds away from muttering, "My precious."

"What can I help you with?" The guy shuts the door and follows me inside.

I don't answer because I'm too distracted by the graffiti covering all four walls in bright colors. There's a group of young kids playing a board game at one of the six-foot tables in the center of the place. Falling in Reverse is blasting from the surround sound. There's a couch with a huge flat screen along the back wall and a stand under it holding every gaming console ever made.

"Miss?"

I can't stop looking around. Haku, the dragon from Spirited Away, hangs from the ceiling and must stretch twenty feet long. There are so many colors and textures around here, it's incredibly stimulating. My artistic heart skips a beat.

"Miss? Did you need something done to your computer or are you consigning it?"

"What?" I finally drag my gaze back to the guy talking to me. "Umm. Yeah. I'm here to see Glitch?" Because this guy isn't Glitch. His voice is way too… normal.

"He's in the back. Hang on." The guy shouts over at the table of kids, "Hey, Beetle! Go tell the boss man someone's here for him."

A kid springs from his seat and dashes into the back.

"That boy has more energy than I get after six quad macchiatos."

"Six quad?"

"Four shots of espresso in each."

Holy shit. "You drink *six* of those a day?"

"Only when I want to speak to electricity and hear colors."

I laugh, and it feels great because I haven't felt this light in weeks.

While I wait for Glitch to appear, I let me eyes, and mind, wander some more.

• • •

Glitch

I can't find a replacement for this one fucking screw, and it's driving me nuts. After taking apart a Zephyrus G15 laptop, I refuse to get it all back together and have one screw beat me. Most people tear this equipment apart and end up with screws left over. Not me. My dumbass managed to lose it, and I can't find my box of spares to save my life.

The back of my shop is made up of an inventory closet and an eight-foot-long worktable that no one else but me can use. Boxes are lined up against one of the walls, and I have tubes of posters in a barrel that I give out as prizes sometimes. Above my tool bench is a series of small drawers with a variety of screws, pins, and spare memory cards. Below that is an old toolbox filled with hard drives, batteries, spare wires, graphics cards, and other shit.

"Uncle Glitch!"

"Yeah?" I call out. Ah-ha! Found it! I pluck a small screw out the drawer and clutch it in my hand as I turn around to see what my nephew needs. He comes here after school on days my sister works evenings. I get stuck helping him with his homework, but I don't mind.

"There's a lady here to see you."

I freeze. *Ara*. I almost gave up hope that she'd actually come. I never gave her a specific day or time to drop into my shop, but in the back of my mind, I really hoped it would have been the next day. When she never showed, I shoved away the possibility of her bringing computer problems to me so I wouldn't fixate on it.

I spent the better part of Monday staring at the door. Tuesday, I came in on my day off and waited in the back, distracting myself by organizing shit. Wednesday, I was a salty motherfucker. This morning I came in thinking she'd gone elsewhere and refused to be upset about it. She didn't know me. I'd never made an effort with her. And it was a computer, not a fucking date. She wasn't standing me up.

But the instant Beetle said a woman was here to see me, damned if my heart didn't leap into my throat. I calmly make my way to the door and look out.

The screw I've spent forty-five minutes trying to find falls out of my hand and bounces across the floor.

Ara's back is to me. Jesus fucking Christ, this woman's ass should be illegal. There's so much I want to grab and bite. My hands close into fists and I grind my molars together. Fuck me, she's hot. And I haven't even seen her face yet. Her pink hair is long and curly, cascading down her back in waves. I imagine digging my fingers into it, tugging by the roots, and forcing her head back so I can kiss her while I take her from behind.

"Are you okay, Uncle Glitch?"

I snap out of my fantasy at the sound of my nephew. Holy shit, I forgot he was here. I forgot *I* was here. Completely sucked into Ara's orbit, I didn't realize there were other life forms around. "Yeah. Why?"

"You're making weird noises."

Am I? Well, he'll get it one day when he's a grown ass man lusting over his perfect woman. I can't peel my gaze away from Ara. She tips her head back and laughs at something my manager says to her. Rage and jealousy have me leaving my sanctuary and heading for the counter.

I don't want anyone else getting a piece of her. Not her laugh. Her time. Her attention.

She's mine.

I can't explain why I feel the way I do, but now that she's here, she's real.

And she's fucking *mine*.

"Glitch, this lady has a computer she needs you to—"

"Ara," I say, and quickly grab the computer from her. I can't believe my manager made her hold this heavy thing. Fucker should be fired for this. I set the equipment on the counter and hold out my hand. As long as she shakes it, I won't use it to choke my manager for calling her a lady. She's a goddess and nothing less. "It's nice to finally meet you."

Ara's eyes widen, and her cheeks turn a bright red.

There it is. The reaction I usually get when I open my mouth. She's heard me talk before, so I don't get why my voice would trigger this response now, but it's starting to make me uneasy. If I can't figure a way to gain control, I'll glitch.

I refuse to let that happen.

But as she gawks at me, with her pretty mouth parted and her pupils blown wide, I start to wonder if she's the one having the glitch. I bunch my brow together. "Are you okay?"

She sways. Her exhale is shaky, and I watch red and pink blotches take over her neck and chest. Which means I'm now staring at her cleavage.

I want to drag my tongue between her tits and fuck them. Cover them in my cum. Bite them.

Fuck me sideways, I'm getting a hard-on.

Damage control. DAMAGE. CONTROL!

"When do you need your computer back?" I think of sports. I think of shit-stained underwear. I think of the night Trey puked all over my suit at our friend's wedding. I think of a million things that should deflate my dick, and none of it works. Especially not when Ara bites her bottom lip.

A growl rises from my throat.

Holy Hell. I've never acted this way before. It's fucking everything up.

"You're Glitch," she finally says.

I rub the back of my neck and wince. "Yeah."

"*Glitch*?"

"Yeah." How much more awkward can we be here? "And you're Ara."

This is painful. Am I not what she thought I'd look like? My body's filled out, so my deep voice goes well with the muscles I work hard for. I'm six-foot-four and have a full sleeve of ink on my left arm. Am I too much? Not enough? Some women don't like dark-haired, inked up men like me.

Ara's gaze lingers on the tattoos covering my forearm. Then her eyes sail across my chest and dip until she...

Yeah, she just checked out my package.

Her cheeks are crimson now. I swear I see a sheen of sweat forming on her forehead.

She likes what she sees.

I arch a brow and clench my molars to keep my smile to a minimum. For once, I'm able to take the reins and drive the first conversation, which is huge for me, honestly. I usually need a minute to warm up to people, but I'm already burning white hot for her.

I run my hand over my mouth, bring her attention upwards. She follows my movements like a cat with a bird.

Heyyyy, Kitty.

"So." I clear my throat. "It randomly shuts down, huh?" She just keeps eating me up with her eyes. They follow my hand as I tap the top of her computer. "Does it make any weird noises too?"

She blinks. "Oh. Yeah. No. Wait… what?"

Adorable.

It takes me two seconds to see the crack and dent in the side. *I'll be damned.* "You actually kicked it?" I thought Trey was joking about that.

Now her face pales. "I didn't."

Tension builds in my shoulders. "But someone did?"

She suddenly looks like she wants to bolt. "I, ummm."

"Here, come with me. Let's talk about this someplace quieter." I don't like that she's shifty. And I don't appreciate an audience.

"Okay," she says quietly, and the boisterous pink-haired bombshell vanishes that fast. A meek, nervous mouse has replaced her. It engages my protective instincts. If she didn't kick her computer, who did and why?

I'm pissed before I even know the answers. Someone damaged Ara's property. Someone destroyed something she loves. They should have a lesson in manners.

I'm more than willing to give that motherfucking lesson.

Placing it gingerly on the table in the back of my shop, I get a better look at it. It's similar to what I have at home. But hers isn't just cracked, it's melted on the inside, and something definitely rattled when I carried it in here.

"Do you want to tell me what happened?" I feel bad for prying, but I want to know.

"No."

I respect her answer. It kills me to not know the details, though. I'll earn her trust and ask again later.

"It caught on fire last night," she blurts. "I tried to restart it one more time and it blew like a firework."

There most likely isn't a way to fix this. "How wedded to this machine are you?" Because I have bad news to give her.

"I..." She bites her lip again. Ara's beauty blows me away. She's the prettiest woman I've ever seen. Brown eyes, big lips, black winged eyeliner, and now that I'm closer, I can see her hair isn't all pink. It has some purple and black streaks, too. *Fucking stunning.* "Is there nothing you can do to save it?"

There's sentimental value attached to this thing, I bet. "I'll do everything in my power to get it running again. But if I can't..."

"It's okay." Something passes over her face that I can't make out, and my heart thuds with an ache seeing it. "I'd just really like to try and save it if it's possible."

Same. "How soon do you need it back?"

"No rush." Ara rubs her neck like she's a little flustered. "And I'll pay for your time, even if it can't be fixed."

She isn't paying me a dime.

"I'll get started on it today." I suspect it's a lost cause, but I don't want to say it without knowing for sure. I've worked on consoles that looked worse, so hey, there might be a chance of salvaging this thing. I'll find out once I tear into it. "I can text you when it's ready." *Or drop it off at your house and worship you for a night.*

She shoots me a killer smile that makes my knees weak. "Yeah, great. I mean, please don't put me at the top of the pile. I'm sure you have a lot going on." She looks past me at the kids playing chess at one of the tables and sighs. "Thanks for this, Glitch."

I love the way she says my name. I want to make her scream it till her throat is raw.

Holy shit, what's wrong with me? I've never been this way over a woman in my life. So ready to drop to my knees and make her feel like she's the only star I'll orbit around. Instead, I'm the computer geek she's entrusting with her broke ass gaming system.

I flash her an easy smile, hoping my vibe will offset the tension in her gaze.

"I'm sure it's a lost cause." She clears her throat. "But I just want to know for sure before I plan burial services for it."

"I've never let technology beat me," I say like a fucking asshat.

My manager slips into the back room with us, inserting himself into the convo, uninvited. "It's true." He grabs a box of candy bars to hand out to the kids. "Glitch is a wizard."

"Well, Wizard. I appreciate this." Ara steps back, and it takes everything in me to not take one step forward to keep our proximity close. She smells good. Looks good. Sounds good.

Bet she tastes amazing.

"I'll text you."

Her gaze lingers on mine for a heartbeat. "Looking forward to it." Ara spins around to leave and stops halfway through the shop. Turning towards me again, she tosses an easy smile my way and I swear my entire shop glows from it. "I'm so glad we've finally met in person, Glitch."

She walks off before I can say something back. It's just as well. All my thoughts jumble and words lodge in my throat as she bumps the door with her fine ass and slips on sunglasses as she heads back to her car.

"Wow," my manager whispers.

I want to throat-punch him.

"She's hot."

He's definitely fired.

"Suuuuuper hot!" says one of the kids at the chess table.

I turn my attention to the middle schoolers and grind my teeth. "Respect, boys. Show some."

I watch her drive off and remind myself I need to practice what I preach.

CHAPTER 5

Ara

Oh my God. Oh my God. Oh. My. God. Glitch is hot, swoony, sexy, fire.

Holy shit. HOLY. FUCKING. SHIT!

The instant I saw him, I was done. Then I heard his deep voice say my name and my body reacted viscerally. My fucking panties are soaked. And I do mean they're sopping wet. I'm going to have to go home and change before I finish running my errands. Holy shit, I even started sweating in front of him. This is so embarrassing.

My creativity didn't touch his level of hotness. It should be criminal to look, sound, and smell that good. It's unfair to the rest of us mere humans.

Glitch has to be a demon. A big, sexy, came-to-fuck-the-soul-out-of-your-body demon.

Holy shit. I can't pull myself together. I've painted pictures in my head of what I thought Glitch would look like. I didn't do him justice. I wasn't even close. He's taller than I thought, built but not bulky, and the ink was everywhere.

Did I mention his dark hair? It curls a little at the ends and looks fun to pull while riding his face.

Wait. No. Stop thinking like that, Ara.

I can't stop. From the instant my name left his sexy fucking mouth, I started imagining the millions of things I wanted to do to him.

He's probably not going to be able to fix my computer. Right now, I don't care. I just want another excuse to see him again. Would it be wrong to throw my laptop off my balcony so he can fix that next?

After I leave Glitch's shop, I drive home on autopilot. I can't stop shaking. I've never been so tongue tied, nervous, turned on, and flabbergasted at the same time before. I legit had an adrenaline rush and he didn't even touch me.

To know I've been talking to this man for months and he looks like *that*? Fuuuuuck.

I'm not worthy. I'm too fluffy for a guy like that. Too broke. Too everything-that's-not-good-enough.

Stop it, Ara. You're better than that. Self-deprecation isn't cool.

I lip-stalled back at the shop with him. I couldn't make words come out of my mouth for the life of me. He probably thinks I'm a tool.

All the bad thoughts start creeping in and it's hard to force them out, but I do because I saw the way he looked at me. There was no disappointment in his expression when he saw me. He actually looked *hungry*. And talk about matching energies. His shop had some of my favorite anime painted on the walls. I wonder who the artist was? Did Glitch paint too?

How much do we actually have in common?

Look, after my last attempted relationship, life's gone downhill. Beyond the sex drought, I barely leave my safe spaces anymore. I've poured all my energy into my art. And what little bit of sex life I have is with me, myself, and an imagination full of Glitch.

I'm not sure what this says about me.

Could he tell I get myself off on fantasies I conjure of us together? *Oh god*. I feel so seen. So transparent and stupid.

Well so what. Maybe he should be flattered that he drives me so wild. Bet I'd make him blush with all the dirty thoughts I have of him and then he'd be the one all hot and bothered, sweating in his shop.

I drive the whole way home, imagining us together — even for one night — and it makes me feel like a dirty girl. I like thinking dirty thoughts. I like doing dirty things. But seeing Glitch in real life has added a new element to my imagination.

Oh my God. He's probably married. If he was mine, I'd put a ring on it. One on his finger and another on his motherfucking cock.

Guys as hot as Glitch do *not* stay single for long. Unless he's a player.

Ugh. He's probably a player.

But a player would have flirted with me online by now, and Glitch never has.

Pull yourself together, Ara. I take a deep breath before heading up to my apartment. Unlocking my door, cool air hits my face and I'm suddenly not interested in running more errands today. I came home to change my outfit — because yes, I'm telling you my panties were that fucking soaked — but now that I'm here, I don't feel like doing anything except touch myself.

I sit on my bed and eye my side table drawer.

My sex drive is out of control and it's all Glitch's fault. If he read the alphabet backwards, he'd make butter melt. I'm softer than butter. And now my fantasies are going next level.

Get a grip, Ara.

I can't.

Pulling my phone out, I text Trey.

Ara: Is Glitch with someone?

I regret my decision to text the instant I send it.

Trey: You mean now or in general?

I roll my eyes.

Ara: Is he in a relationship with anyone?

I watch the little dots appear as he types his response and my pulse races.

Trey: Nope.

Ara: Okay. Thanks.

I know he's going to press me, but I really hope he doesn't.

Trey: You interested?

Damnit.

Ara: I was just curious.

Trey: K

He leaves it at that, thank God.

I glance over at my laptop. I'm totally tossing it out the window to get Glitch to look at it next. The fact that he can fix shit is another turn on for me. Guys with big brains are even hotter than guys with big dicks. Glitch, I'm pretty sure, has both.

Jesus, I stared at his cock earlier in the shop. I legit gawked at his fucking package and I'm pretty sure he caught me doing it.

Get it together, Ara. Distract yourself.

I chew on my lip and check my email for the tenth time today. I've been hoping to hear back about a commission piece soon. It takes me three seconds to see they haven't responded yet. *Damnit.* It's just as well. My muse is still hiding. Has been since before my breakup.

My cell rings, and I frown at the screen. *Unknown.*

It can't be Glitch already, could it? This isn't his cell number, but maybe it's the shop? "Hello?"

Heavy breathing on the other end makes my blood run cold.

"Jason. If this is you, you have to stop."

More heavy breathing.

I hang up. I've blocked him, but he finds ways around it. So far, he hasn't shown up at my studio, but it hasn't stopped me from jumping whenever I hear a knock on my door there or at home. The problem with Jason is I'm not sure he'd knock before busting his way inside.

The man has a temper and a jealous streak I never saw coming.

Good fucking riddance.

I stare at the laptop sitting on my desk, opposite my bed. I should get rid of it. I don't know why I haven't yet. I guess because it works, and it's a decent back up if I need it. But Jason gave it to me, and I hate it on principal. I hate him.

Focus on Glitch.

Backing away from resentment and anger, I go where my safe space is in my head. Now that I've experienced the real man, it's easy to conjure him in my mind. I lean back on my bed and close my eyes. I focus on the details of Glitch's face that I've already committed to memory and pretend he uses that sensual mouth to say dirty things to me.

"Let me see that pretty pussy. Mmmm. Bet you taste so good."

I pull my jeans and panties off, kicking them away.

Glitch's mouth is sinful. He flashes me a smile that I've also committed to memory. White teeth, devilish grin. I pretend he tips his head to the side, eyeing me like he can't decide what part of my body he wants to fuck first.

"You need my cock, don't you?"

Yes. I. Do.

I've never experienced arousal like this before. It's borderline embarrassing.

"You're so wet for me, Kitty."

I tighten my thighs, fighting the urge to seek better friction. Like I said, my appetite is insatiable. But for once, I want to hold out a little.

"Open your thighs wide for me." He growls with appreciation. *"I love how wet you get. This is mine. Say it. Fucking say who owns this pussy."*

"You," I whisper before biting my lip.

The phone vibrates next to my leg, startling me.

Holy shit, it's Glitch! I can't make my body uncoil enough to answer without hitting the button five fucking times. "H-hello?" I'm shaking. Talk about a head rush. My cheeks heat, and I press my hands to them. I'm so glad we're not on Facetime.

"Hey, Ara."

My heart runs panicked circles in my chest. "Hey." I clear my throat and sit up. "Any luck?"

"Afraid not. I was able to salvage some parts, but I'm not comfortable giving them back without testing each one first to make sure they don't catch fire too."

I get all warm and gooey inside. See? This is what I mean about Glitch being safe. He says things — or types them — that make me feel protected.

"I'll make sure all pieces are boxed up beautifully... for the burial."

I laugh and it comes out so husky and awkward. I want to die. "I'll write an obit."

"Mmmph. I can set up flower arrangements."

"Wonderful."

Did I mention my hand is still between my thighs? I can't seem to move it away, and I don't want to rub my clit on the phone with him. I need to get off. Points for the double entendre, please. "Okay. Umm. I can pick it up tomorrow, then."

"Or I can drop it off tonight."

It wasn't a question.

"Sure." I hope my voice doesn't give my excitement away. "I'll text you the address."

"Perfect." Glitch's tone matches mine, and I swear I hear his smile.

"Perfect." Wait. I... he... shit, I sound like a parrot. "Okay well..."

"I'm sorry I couldn't fix it." He genuinely sounds like he feels bad about it.

"It's not a big deal."

"See you soon." He hangs up first and I panic. Instead of getting myself off, I beeline it to the bathroom. I get halfway there before I trip on my own good senses and pitch forward, arms pinwheeling. I don't catch my balance in time and end up skidding on my knees across the floor. "Ouch!" I rub my knees and feel so silly.

I don't know why I'm this giddy. He's just coming to give me back my broke ass pile of computer pieces. He's not coming in. He's not taking me out. We're not fucking. He probably won't even stay for longer than five minutes.

So, I'm going to make sure that for those five minutes I look good enough to eat.

CHAPTER 6

Glitch

When my sister texted earlier saying she was already home, I closed up shop and gave everyone the rest of the evening off, then took my nephew home.

Beetle drops his bookbag and kicks off his shoes the instant he's through the door. The house smells like spaghetti and garlic bread. My stomach rumbles because I haven't had anything other than a granola bar since ten this morning. I find my sister in the kitchen by the stove.

"Thanks for dropping him off." Erin taps her wooden spoon against the pot. "You wanna to stay for dinner?"

"Nah, I got some place to be."

"Ohhhh a date?"

"You wish." Erin's always bugging me about my love life. Hers is just as lame. "He finished his homework already, and I signed the field trip forms and added it to the family calendar." I turn to leave, eager to get to Ara.

"Glitch?"

"Yeah?"

"Thank you."

I flash her a big smile. Helping my sister take care of Beetle is an honor. His father bolted the minute he found out Erin was pregnant, and we've never seen him since. Such a piece of shit. If I can be a good role model for Beetle, I will.

"I have off tomorrow, so he won't have to come to the shop after school."

That's weird. "You got home early today and have off tomorrow? What gives?" *Don't say it. Don't say it.*

"I got let go."

Shit. "I have some money stashed. If you need it—"

"No. It's fine." Erin waves me off. "I knew this was coming and have been preparing."

"You're sure?"

"Yeah. If I run into a pinch, I'll let you know."

"Promise?"

"Mmm hmm." She will. We're open and honest about everything.

And maybe losing this position is a good thing. Erin hated her job and only stayed because it paid the bills. I can't count how many times I've encouraged her to look elsewhere. I get that not everyone can afford the luxury of finding a job they love, but no one should be stuck wasting away in a position they hate either. My sister's been stuck for forever. First, taking care of me when our parents died, and then her son. I don't envy single moms. Erin's been one since she was a fucking kid.

"Beetle!" I holler.

He looks over from the couch. "Yeah?"

"Help your mom with the dishes tonight, okay?"

"Okay."

Love you, Erin mouths at me.

"Love you too."

I rush back to my car and double check Ara's address on my phone. Her box of computer parts sits on my passenger seat, and I can't help but feel bad about it. I've already ordered a brand-new system, which she won't know about until I get it all together.

It takes me less than five minutes to reach her apartment. I can't believe she lives this close to me and my family.

Set in a cluster, the apartment complex has one central parking lot with shitty lighting. I don't like it. This is one of the oldest developments in the neighborhood and it needed work when *I* was a kid. Scanning the area, I spot a few boys kicking a ball in the grass as a woman talks on her cell, half-ass watching them. Two guys are over by their cars talking to each other. The bushes need trimming, and the sidewalk is uneven, and it makes me worry Ara would trip. I grab the box and head to building A. The lobby door is unlocked. I don't like that either.

Why am I being so protective of a woman I barely know?

Doesn't matter why. I just am, and that's all there is to it.

I make it to the third floor fast. Her door is on the left.

Knock, knock.

I hold her box close to my ribs and run a hand through my hair to smooth it back.

The door swings open.

I lose my breath.

"Hi."

"Hi." Fuck me sideways. Ara looks spectacular. For whatever reason, her earlier outfit has been replaced with a maxi dress. I only know that's what they're called because Erin has a closest full of them.

I hold the box up. "Rest in pieces."

Ara laughs, and it vibrates down my spine. "Want to come in?"

What a loaded question that is. "Absolutely."

She steps out of my way, ushering me inside. Her place is cute and cheery. Tiny and clean. It smells like oranges.

"So, what do I owe you?"

It takes me a second to understand what she just asked. "Nothing."

"Come on, Glitch. Don't do that."

"Don't do what?" I set the box down and shove my hands in my pockets.

"You helped me out. *And* you delivered it to my house. I owe you something for your effort."

I can think of a million ways she could repay me, and none of them include a dollar figure. "No, it's fine. Really."

"*Glitch.*" She regards me with an incredulous look that I'd love to kiss off her face. "Seriously. You have a business and I'm your customer. At least let me pay you for your time."

"Dinner." My time is all hers. And I'm not hurting for business.

"Excuse me?"

"I want to take you to dinner. That's what I want as payment." The rest of what I want can wait.

Her cheeks turn bright pink. "Okay."

My smile goes a mile wide. "Where would you like to go?"

"You mean *now*?"

This date is long overdue, if I'm being honest. "Now sounds good to me. Unless…" I slowly close the gap between us, "you've eaten already." The moment I say it, I know she has. Some people are easy to read and Ara's definitely one of them.

"I had a late lunch." She tucks her hair behind her ear. "But we can still go out. I can grab something light."

"I don't want you to eat light." God help me, but even I catch how much my register drops as I talk to her. "I want you ravenous."

Her pupils blow wide.

I love how responsive she is to me. It makes me want to say a million dirty things to her. I wonder what she'd do if I did?

CHAPTER 7

Ara

Wearing a maxi dress was a big mistake. I'm wet. If I sit, it's going to show. I'd forgone underwear because… well…

Like I said, big mistake.

Glitch is staring at me like he wants *me* for dinner. And he's got green eyes with blue and yellow flecks in them that seem to darken the more I stare. He sucks in his bottom lip, and my eyes drift to his mouth. Jesus, this man is fine.

Dressed in a dark gray t-shirt and jeans, he looks both dangerous and unassuming at the same time. He pulls his hands out of his pockets and I glance at his ink. There are so many images curving around his muscles, it's amazing.

Out of nowhere, I hear his stomach growl. Loudly. Now I feel terrible for not just lying to him and saying, *Yes, take me to dinner now. I'm starving!* "What do you want to eat?"

He smiles at me wickedly. "You."

Holy Hell. I don't think he's lying. Heat floods my body and it's hard to breathe. *You can do this, Ara. You can totally do this.* Look, talking trash to your friends online over a game is not the same as talking dirty to a man you've been fantasizing over and getting off on for months.

But I'm going to try my best.

I step closer and press my hand to his chest. Holy wow, his body is hard. The steady, strong beat of his heart thuds against my palm. He's not nervous like me. I'm glad. One of us needs to be in control here, and I know it won't be me. I'll fuck it up.

I lick my lips and love that he watches. "Me?" I tease breathlessly. "I might be too much for you."

"Only one way to find out." He leans in and waits for me to meet him in the middle. His gaze is playful and primal at the same time. It's like staring at a panther who can't decide what he wants to do with his mouse. Glitch brings his hand to the back of my head, threading his fingers into my hair, and brings me closer, closer, closer.

Then his stomach growls extra loud and I start laughing.

"Wow." He grabs his belly. "I've legit never been cockblocked by myself before."

The tension between us eases enough for me to take in some air. "Let's get you some food." I head into my kitchen, feeling Glitch's gaze on my ass as I go.

It does look dynamite in this dress. These things are incredibly forgiving while still hella flattering. "I have…" Opening my fridge, I quickly slam it shut. "Ramen or cereal. And a half jar of pickles."

"Ramen's good."

I can't believe I'm going to make this man fucking *ramen*. Just shoot me now. "I haven't been to the grocery store in forever." Now I'm flustered. "I don't eat much while I'm painting, so I never think to get food until it's too late." I grab the last pack I have, but before I can open it, Glitch takes it from me.

"Come on." He places the ramen back in the cupboard and grabs my hand, luring me out of the kitchen.

"Where are we going?" Because my bedroom is in the opposite direction of where he's pulling me.

"Out."

"Okay." I snag my keys from the little table by my door and follow him. I can't help the cheesy grin I'm rocking. And the fact that I so easily and quickly follow his lead is alarming. I swear he could lure me into Hell, and I'd joyfully skip the whole way down.

He leans against the wall, hands stuffed in his pockets again as I lock up. "That dress is phenomenal on you, Ara."

I bite my lip to keep from squealing. I seriously have no chill. "Where to?"

"You'll see."

I follow Glitch to his car, and he opens the door for me while simultaneously looking around the parking lot. I swear he's searching for predators. Even after he shuts my door, he's still looking around like he expects trouble. This complex is old and crappy, but affordable. The outside's a little creepy, but my apartment is great. Okay, not great, but decent. It's enough for me.

"Buckled up?" he asks, dropping into the driver's seat.

Yes, Daddy. "Yeah."

"Sorry," he lightly chuckles. "I uhhhh… I'm used to having a kid in the car with me. I say shit out of habit."

He has a kid? "How old are they?"

"He's nine." Glitch freezes. "It's my nephew. Not my kid. I don't have any kids."

I'm not sure how to respond. "Cool." Cool. *COOL?* Christ on a cracker! I need a lesson on how to be sexier.

Starting the engine, he grinds his molars, which only flexes his jaw muscles.

Because of course he has a sharp jaw line too.

And don't get me going on his forearms or how hot he looks backing out of the parking spot, spinning the wheel with the heel of his palm.

Wow, Ara. Doesn't take much to make you swoon. I have got to get laid. I swear everything I see my brain makes sexual.

To my surprise, we pull up to a grocery store. Glitch cuts the engine and slaps my thigh. "Come on."

I love that we keep finding ways to touch each other. It's more him than me. He grabs a cart and heads for the produce aisle first. "Apples?"

Love them. "Yeah. Ummm. Are we seriously grocery shopping on our first date?"

He flashes another killer grin. "We're *preparing* for our first date."

"Fuji, gala, and honeycrisp."

He bags three of each. "Grapes?"

"Red," I say, then watch him put green and red in the cart.

"Ohhhh, strawberries." He grabs a couple of boxes and heads to the veggies for some carrots. We joke and make our way down each aisle. I end up pushing the cart because I need something to keep my body busy. Glitch walks beside me sometimes, and behind me, others. We work our way through the entire store until the cart is filled.

"This is a lot for one dinner."

He just smiles, placing everything on the conveyer belt in a meticulous way. He must catch the expression on my face because he says,

"I used to be a bagger when I was in high school. There's a method to this."

I don't doubt it. "You seem like someone who has a method to everything."

He winks, and I want to squeal again.

The chemistry between us is wild. Like we've been together forever, but it's also brand new and exciting. He's easy to be around. And his confidence is wonderful. Comfortable.

I slap a baguette on top of the frozen pizza. He grabs it, but I don't let go of my end. We glower playfully, and I realize I want to mess with him. I like the fiery look in his eyes when I do.

He leans into me and growls, "Brat."

He knew that about me already. I never hold my tongue when we play online, and it's time I learn to not hold back in all aspects of my life. "Whatcha gonna do about it?"

He drags his eyes down my body. "Fuck around and find out."

I'm on fire.

Glitch hovers his phone over the scanner, paying for the food before I can even get my credit card out. We've bought a ton of groceries, and I know it's not all for tonight's dinner date. No one can eat five pizzas, six apples, four pounds of chicken, ramen, oatmeal, a variety of fruit, and a two-pound bag of skittles in one night.

I keep my mouth shut and smile at the cashier when she hands me the receipt. Glitch snags it from me before I catch the total, and the computer's already back to the home screen, so I can't see it there either. Damnit.

"So, how long have you lived here?"

"My whole life," he says. We yip-yap all the way back to my apartment. He's easy to talk to. It's like we've been friends for forever.

Finally home, Glitch makes it his goal to hook every bag around his arms because he refuses to make more than one trip, or let me help. I lead the way, hold the lobby door open, and then rush up the steps to beat him to my apartment. I unlock fast and he blazes in, bags strung around both arms and two more dangling from his fingers.

"Here, let me take some."

He growls playfully and sweeps past me to put them on the counter. "Phew." He stretches his arms over his head. The act makes his shirt ride up enough for me to catch a glimpse of more ink on his abs. "I didn't think I was going to win that one."

"Milk almost got you?"

"The bread," he corrects. "I nearly crushed the baguette coming up the second flight of steps."

We start laughing, and I pull out the chicken. "What are we making with this?" I hadn't asked earlier.

"Whatever you want. That's for later this week."

I freeze. Then I take a real good look at this food. "You bought me groceries for the week." I'm not mad. I'm mortified.

"I bought dinner."

"You bought me groceries." I don't know if I want to laugh or cry or hide under a rock. "I can pay for my own fucking food, Glitch."

I shove the chicken in the fridge and snag the next thing and shove that in the freezer. I think it was the peas. I can't even tell because I'm all flustered.

"Hey." Glitch grabs both my hands and stops me. "I bought dinner for the week. And some snacks."

I look at all the bags. "Well…" I can't figure out how to feel. I knew what he was doing in the store, and I let it happen. I just hadn't expected him to pay at the end. "I guess you'll be here a lot this week since you've bought enough food to make six huge dinners."

"See?" He grins. "You were right about me, Ara. I do have a method for everything."

I shouldn't like this. In fact, I should pay him back and tell him it was nice to run an errand, and that I'll see him around. But I don't want to. Honestly, this is the sweetest thing anyone's done for me in a long time. "You're trying to take care of me," I accidentally say out loud.

He tenses with the box of cereal in his hand and slowly puts it in the cupboard. "I've overstepped."

"No." Maybe a little. "I'm glad you did this." I hand him more things to shove in the cupboards. "It's probably one of the nicest things anyone's ever done for me."

We stare at each other again. "The bar must be low if buying you a baguette is considered one of the nicest things someone's ever done for you."

The look in his eyes, paired with the tension in his shoulders, melts me a little. I need to recover some power here. "Hasn't anyone ever told you, the way to a girl's heart is through carbs?" I grab the baguette and run my hand down the length. "It's a pretty decent size too, but I've had bigger."

The intensity leaves his gaze, and he smiles again. "The bakery must have been cold. It'll be more impressive once it's warmed up."

I playfully whack him on the arm with it. He takes it from me and tosses it to the counter, then grabs me by the waist. We close in on each other. We're going to kiss. I hold my breath. He leans in and his mouth almost brushes mine.

Smack!

I'm instantly reeling, my mouth wide open. "You *spanked* me!"

"That's for being a brat in the grocery store."

He's not sorry. Neither am I.

Oh my God, this guy is fun.

Glitch snags the Skittles off the counter and rips the bag open with his teeth. Pouring some candy into his hand, he holds a green one out for me to take.

If this is my reward, he better give me something bigger than that. I open my mouth, lean in, and bite down on his fingers.

CHAPTER 8

Glitch

She bit me!

All the blood rushes to my dick the instant her mouth wraps around the Skittle between my fingers, and when she chomps down, the pain is hard and sharp and oh so fucking delicious.

I'd expect nothing less from a dirty mouthed firecracker of a goddess like Ara.

I think I'm in love.

No. I *know* I'm in love. I have been for months and spending an hour perusing the grocery store, buying her a bunch of her favorite foods only maddens my heart more. I want to provide for and protect her. Worship her morning, noon, and night. The thought of anyone else doing it makes me murderous.

That I haven't ripped that damn dress off her by now shows how well-behaved I'm trying to be.

Biting my finger just broke the leash I'd put on myself.

I pull my finger out of her mouth and laugh. "It's not nice to bite." Yes, it is.

"You're lucky I didn't do worse." Ara snags the bag of Skittles from my hand. "That'll teach you to hold back on me." She dumps a bunch into her mouth at once.

"So it's like that, huh?"

Ara shrugs as she grinds down on her sugar. "You can't just feed me one of these at a time. That's torture."

That's not torture. What she's wearing is fucking torture.

Her light gray dress hugs her curves and flaunts all her assets as well as showcases her neediness. I had to bite back my urges the entire time we were at the grocery store when I saw she had a fucking wet spot in the back. I secretly relished the view and coveted it, which was why I walked behind her whenever someone else came within range of seeing it at the store.

I'm not sure if Ara's always this turned on, but I'll lie to myself and say it's because of me.

"You're trying to take care of me." Did she need someone to take care of her? I volunteer. Did she want someone to make sure all her needs were met? I. Vol. Un. Teer.

You learn a lot playing video games with people. And I'm a great listener. Ara's been part of our group for a while and she's always spouting off at the mouth. Sometimes things sneak through her filter. I love catching it when it happens. It's like getting a peek behind a curtain. But now I don't want a glimpse, I want the entire view.

There's a bizarre chemistry between us that's somewhere between shiny/new and old/familiar. It's like we've known each other for a lifetime and yet, I really don't know as much as I'd like about her.

Which is about to change.

I plan to spend as much time with Ara as I can. All this food could easily be dinner for us for a week. Or she could eat it all herself, which would make me twice as happy, because the thought of her going all day with no food doesn't sit well with me.

She's got a gorgeous body, and someone needs to take care of it.

I volunteer.

She throws a Skittle at my head, snapping me out of my glitchy-thoughts.

"*One*," I warn, hoping she catches the humor in my deep tone. "You've just earned *one*."

"One what?"

"Fuck around and find out."

Her smile matches mine. It almost hurts my cheeks. God, this woman is fun.

"Oh, let's not stop at one then." She plucks a strawberry out of the box and throws it at me. "Two." She tosses a grape at me next, and it bounces off my chest. "Three."

I love her. I love her. I love her.

Ara reaches for an apple and rears it back like a baseball. I stand there and wait for it, elated that she's so fiery. "Nah. I'm not bruising it just for a spanking."

She knows what the counts are for. Fuck. Me. This woman is perfect.

Ara puts the honeycrisp back and grabs the baguette again, pitching it at me like a javelin.

I catch it with ease and toss it over my shoulder. I have no clue where it lands. Don't care. All that matters is the beauty in front of me, pouring more candy in her mouth.

I close the space between us. Her lips are wet, breath sticky sweet, cheeks bright pink like her hair. I want to say a million things to her. Confess shit. Drop to my knees, lift her dress, and seal my mouth to her pussy and make her scream my name.

I can see her arousal. She wants me as bad as I want her.

So why am I hesitating?

Maybe it's the fact that her hand is between us, pressing against my pounding heart, holding me back a little.

"I…" She suddenly pales.

Taking the Skittles away, I place them on the counter while keeping my gaze locked on hers. "You?"

"This is not a rebound."

I arch an eyebrow. "It isn't?"

"No."

I can feel the heat radiating off her palm. When she steps back from me, my heart falls to my feet. "Are you sure?"

"Positive." Ara adamantly shakes her head, easing the tightness that's formed in my gut. "I just…" She looks away from me, casting her gaze to the floor. "I for real have no clue why I even just said that. It just flew out of my mouth."

"It's okay." But there's a reason she blurted it, and I want to know why. "Are you and Jason really over this time? For good?" I've lost track of how many times they've broken up. It was the rockiest relationship, and it never made sense to me. You either work or you don't. If you work, enjoy it for however long it lasts. If you don't work, move on.

Ara and Jason would break up, get back together. Break up, get back together. It was frustrating as Hell, especially since I didn't think she liked him all that much to begin with. Then again, we didn't discuss super personal shit on Discord, and I never pried.

"Oh, I'm over him. I'm soooo over him." Ara's voice is shaky. I don't like it.

"Really?"

"Absolutely."

Then why bring this up? "I feel like I'm missing something here, Ara." She's so flustered, I wish I hadn't pushed it. I back away a little bit and lean casually against her wall, so she doesn't feel trapped. "He kicked your computer, didn't he?"

Her cheeks blaze. Her eyes fill with tears.

"He wasn't a good boyfriend," she says quietly. "But it was partly my fault."

Not sure what that means, so I tread carefully. "Under no circumstances should someone destroy your things, Ara. I don't give a shit what you think you did to deserve it."

"He was really jealous." Ara tucks her hair behind her ears. "All the time."

"Of?"

"You."

My heart stops. "Excuse me?"

"I… I'm… he knew I gamed with you guys whenever I could. But I only do it because I like our conversations on Discord."

Our bland, generic, safe conversations. I swear the air evaporates from my lungs.

"He'd get jealous if I paid more attention to you guys than him. Between gaming with you and spending all my time in my studio, he pitched a fit one night and yelled about how he wants more from me. I didn't want to give him more. He took it out on my computer. Which is better than trashing my studio, I guess, but—"

I'm so furious I see red. "Did he ever lay a hand on you?"

"No."

I work really fucking hard to keep my tone calm and soft. Then I close some distance between us. "Are you sure?"

"Yes." She's not lying. I can feel it. "He just started to get super obsessive. The more I worked or did things for myself, the needier he got. I couldn't stand it. When he broke my computer, that was the last straw. It was the first and only time he was violent around me, and I didn't stick around to give him a chance to escalate."

I grab her shoulders and pull her in tight to my chest. "I wish you'd told me sooner."

"I don't know you," she mumbles.

"You know me, Ara." I tip her chin up. "And even if you don't know me well enough yet, you could have gone to Trey."

"I handled it."

And I'm so proud of her for sticking up for herself and knowing her worth. No one should be treated like that. Jason is a dick.

Ara cringes at me. "I'm just going to come out and say it all, okay?"

Fuck, there's more?

"He was jealous of you because he caught me saying your name once."

Oh shit.

"While I was coming."

Oh. Double. Shit.

"Yeah. Sooo…" She pushes away from me and puts her hands on her hips. "How's that for an ending to our first date?"

I stare at her for a few beats. "Who said this is the ending?" I grab her by the ass and pull her in. "This first date's only just begun."

CHAPTER 9

Ara

Glitch's intense gaze doesn't intimidate me, it empowers me. What is it about this guy that makes me so bold?

Everything. The answer is everything.

I've just laid my truth out—or most of it, at least—and I fully expected him to run out of here. Instead, he looks more committed to this evening than before.

I can't believe I told him I got caught saying his name while I came. See, this is what happens when I get flustered. I overshare. But I want him to know because I want him to understand that this isn't a rebound.

I've been harboring secret feelings for him for months. I want to tell him I tried to break up with Jason multiple times because my heart wasn't his, it was Glitch's, and I only kept taking that douche canoe back because I felt guilted into it every time.

That was my fault. I won't ever make that mistake again.

Just like I won't hold back from Glitch tonight, or any other night from here on out.

I back up, making him follow me out of the kitchen, down the hall, and into my bedroom. If we're moving fast, it doesn't feel like it. Honestly, this night feels like it's been in the works for ages.

"It smells so good in here," he says, looking around, taking in every little detail of my personal space. The contrast between his dark hair and inked skin against my blush pink walls and cream bedding is hot. He plucks a white peony from a vase and smells it. Dropping his hand down to his side, he twirls the stem between his fingers and stalks over to me.

I keep walking until the back of my knees hit the bed.

"Promise me something." He buries a hand in my hair and brings me close to his mouth. "If you need me, you'll tell me. Whatever it is, no matter the time of day or night, if you need me, you'll tell me."

The word tumbles off my tongue. "Promise."

Tension eases from his shoulders.

I thought he'd push me onto the bed next, but that's not what Glitch does. He presses me flush against his chest, spins me around, and walks me back to the bare wall next to my dresser.

Our eyes deadlock.

My heart hammers in my chest.

"Ara, I'm about to say something that's going to come out really, really fucked."

I can't wait. "Spill it."

"I'm glad your computer's broken."

I don't know how to respond, because honestly, me too.

"It got us here, and I'm glad it did. But I'm pissed I can't fix it. I should have been able to fix it."

He's not talking about the computer. I know he's not, because his tone is restrained and his hands tremble on my hips.

"I'm glad it broke too," I say, swallowing my pride. I built that damn thing with some of the money I earned off my very first commission. It meant big things for me. It meant I was successful and could spoil myself a little. Since I'm in a dry spell now, with no new money in sight, a massive creative block, failed relationships that were total nightmares, and up until today I didn't even have food in my pantry, I'd put more meaning on that stupid piece of equipment than I should have. "I'm glad you had that chat room open all the time for us."

"Me too." *I wish you'd have used it and told me about Jason sooner.* He didn't say those words, but they were there, hanging in the air between us.

Glitch always kept the channel between us private. It was open for me anytime I wanted to pop in and say something. I just rarely did. Not nearly as often as I wanted to, at least. But knowing the option was there, that the door was open, had been a comfort. Weird, right?

"Glitch?" I snake my hand around his neck.

"Hmm?"

"Want to reboot?"

The air whooshes out of him, and he laughs. "Yeah. Let's do that."

A do over would be great, right about now. "Okay. How?"

He smashes his mouth to mine, erasing every coherent thought from my head. I swear I'm floating. Blood rushes to my ears and I'm a little dizzy. Holy fuck, this man can kiss.

"Hi," I say once he lets me go.

Glitch radiates confidence. His eyes gleam with desire. To be the center of his attention is like I'm the sun he orbits around. And I'm burning. He leans into the side of my face and runs his nose up my cheek. His breath is hot against the shell of my ear when he growls, "Heyyy, Kitty."

Swear to fuck, my eyes roll back in ecstasy. Two words. Two fucking words are all it takes for me to lose my composure. The butterflies in my belly are now a fireball of tight need coiling inside me. I keep my eyes closed and clutch my throat. *Breathe. Breathe. Breathe.*

Glitch brackets his hands on the wall by my head. His mouth rubs against the shell of my ear again, making my nipples harden into tight peaks. "Take your dress off for me and show me what I've been missing out on."

I hesitate.

"Four," he counts, nuzzling my neck. "Want to make it five?"

I don't move.

"Five it is." Glitch places a gentle kiss on my neck—the polar opposite of the spankings I'm earning by disobeying his commands.

"You want it off, do it yourself."

"Six," he counts, even as he gathers the fabric, bunching it inch by inch in his hands. He cocks a brow and focuses on rucking my dress higher and higher. Fuck counting, he can spank me till I can't sit for all I care. I just don't ever want this to stop. He tugs the dress over my head and now sees I don't have on panties.

He bunches my dress into his hands and brings a specific—and suspiciously wet—spot up to his nose and inhales. "Fuuuuck, Ara." He tosses the dress to the floor and steps back, appreciating the view.

I'm so glad I wore a good push-up bra today.

There's a massive bulge in his jeans, which further spurs my confidence.

"You look good enough to eat."

I feel hot everywhere his gaze lingers. "Well, you still haven't had dinner."

He runs his thumb across his bottom lip and keeps staring at me.

It starts to make me second guess myself. "Not what you thought?" I've gained some weight lately. Not that he knows that.

"No." He rubs his chin. "So much better."

I release a shaky breath.

"Now where were we?" Glitch backs away and drops down on the edge of my bed. Tilting his head, he stares at every inch of my body. Finally, his gaze lifts to my eyes, and he pats his lap. "Come here, Kitty."

Kitty. He's called me Kitty twice now. I love it so much I could squeal. Instead, I stand there, uncertain of which direction to sit.

Glitch makes the decision for me by turning me so my back is pressed against his chest. It's the best angle, I soon realize, for his mouth to be close to my ear again. His velvet voice is intoxicating when he growls. That's it. That's all he does. Growls. And my lust cranks up ten more notches.

It's starting to feel like a sauna in here.

"I've been fantasizing about you for so long, Ara." His hands drift up my thighs, ribs, then he leans back to run his fingertips along my spine.

The clasp in my bra springs open. I tug the damn thing off and toss it across the room.

"Exquisite." He palms my tits with his hot hands. I want him to pinch my nipples, but I can't bring myself to say it.

When he skates his hands down my torso, I shudder. Everything feels hot and cold at the same time. I can't believe we're here, doing this.

Glitch gathers my hair in his hands and winds it around his palm like a rope. He doesn't pull, just... holds it. "Is there anything I should stay clear of doing to you, Ara?"

Fuuuuck. "I don't think so." I'll let him do anything he wants. My brain can't wrap around a hard line, and I swear it's because I've already put my all my trust in him that he'd never hurt me. I'm an adventurous girl, and there are a ton of things I still haven't tried but want to. The prospect of doing any of those things with Glitch makes my pussy clench with need.

"Are there any places on your body that are off limits?"

My heart clashes into my ribs. "No." I mean it. "But I have one condition."

He nuzzles against my neck and gently bites the spot above my shoulder that drives me wild. "Only one?"

"Mmm hmm." My head falls back on his shoulder. I already feel like I'm in another dimension with his hands all over me like this.

"You better tell me before I start... which is in about two more seconds." He pinches my nipples and I groan, shoving harder into his chest.

"Kitty." I start panting. "I want you to keep calling me Kitty."

His rumbling groan is one-thousand percent primal in response to my demand.

Game on.

CHAPTER 10

Glitch

RIP me. I swear I've died and gone to some fantastical realm where all my wildest fantasies keep coming true.

I feel a little exposed. I've called her Kitty twice tonight, both of which were slip ups. The fact that she loves it makes me feel some kind of way about the audio recordings I've made. Is this Karma? If so, Karma loves me.

She's straddling my thigh, her back to my chest, head leaning on my shoulder. In one fell swoop, this woman became putty in my hands. She trusts me. And though I'm eager to accept the fact that she thinks she has no boundaries, I'm not about to go too fast and prove otherwise. I want to explore Ara. Learn her body. Memorize every squeak, whimper, groan, and sound she makes.

I want her to come so many times, she can't speak.

I want her to fucking *glitch*.

"Rub yourself on my leg, Kitty." Her skin is soft under my fingers as I slide my hands down her thighs and gently pry them open more. I can feel how wet she is through my jeans. She leans forward a little, obeying. I gather her hair up in my hand again. I don't pull it yet. Just hold it like a leash.

"Do you touch yourself often?" I'm sure she does.

"All the time."

"Show me how you do it." I let go of her hair, breathing in the scent of her shampoo before her pink waves fall over her shoulders to cover her tits. Then I lean back to give her more room to move. "Close your eyes and make yourself come like I'm not here."

If she wants to be called Kitty, she'll have to earn it.

Ara shocks me when she stares at our reflection. *So she knows why I chose this seat on her bed.* Her closet is straight ahead of us. There's one of those long mirrors mounted to it, giving us both a front seat to the Ara show. I cock my brow, letting her know I'm waiting.

And counting.

She bites her lip and stares at me through the reflection. Then shoves her middle finger in her mouth, a wicked little flare burning in her gaze, and she licks it like a cat, dragging her tongue from base to tip of her finger. *That's seven.* The fact that she knows she's being a brat and will be spanked accordingly is fantastic. I'm going to make sure she enjoys every fucking one.

Ara touches her clit first, rubbing in tight, tiny circles over the nub. Her cheeks are already flushed. Eyelids hooded. "Scootch back, please."

Curiosity piqued, I oblige.

Ara digs her heels into the mattress, knees dropping wide as she pushes her back against my chest and straddles my lap. Fuck, I love this. She's not shy at all when she shoves her fingers into her pussy and starts finger fucking herself next. The wet noises alone are to die for. My cock strains against my jeans, the zipper biting into me, but I barely notice. Ara has my undivided attention.

Her breaths quicken. She pivots and now I understand why she wanted me further back on the bed. It's to give her more room. Straddling my thigh, Ara swings her legs behind her and rubs her clit harder, faster in this reverse cowgirl position. Squeezing her eyes shut, her face squinches up as she brings herself closer to an orgasm.

I don't say a fucking word.

Nothing to encourage. Nothing to distract.

I'm not sure how long I can stay silent. Or keep my hands to myself.

"Glitch." My name punches out of her like she's desperate for me. Her thighs tighten around my mine as she grinds against my leg. "I'm gonna come."

"Such good girl, Kitty."

She whimpers and rubs her clit harder, faster. Ara's breathtaking when she comes all over my thigh. Her body shudders and I stroke her ass with both my hands while she sucks in ragged breaths and comes down from her head rush.

I take advantage of the situation and spank her three times.

Smack! Smack! Smack!

Ara's guttural groan unravels me. She's still working her clit, already chasing a second release. I spank her two more times and rub her reddened cheeks to soothe the sting. She comes again, but it's not nearly as hard as the first time.

I grab her hair, loving that her back has a sheen of sweat on it already, and wrap her beautiful pink tendrils around my hand again. I gently pull, forcing her to reposition herself. Her back is against my chest, knees bent, tits swaying as she continues breathing hard.

"Give me a taste," I order.

With a lopsided grin, she shoves a finger back into her cunt, slicking it with her cream before pulling out. She holds her middle finger up at me again. It's glistening. I suck it into my mouth, down to the last knuckle, twirling my tongue around and around, making sure I get every drop, before I let it pop out of my mouth.

Ara's tone is sultry. "I've never been able to come... without assistance... before."

She's all kinds of blissed out and breathless. I hope she can handle more because I haven't even started.

"What's it normally take for you to get off?"

She leans over, and her ass goes directly into my face. Fuck, I want to bite and lick her until she's screaming. My girl digs through her bedside table drawer and pulls out a vibrator.

Nice.

"Let me have it." I hold my hand out.

Ara hesitates. Something flashes in her eyes, and I can't pinpoint what it is. But she gives me the vibrator like a good girl anyway.

"Lay back on your pillow."

Another expression flitters across her face.

I cock my brow again in warning. She's down to two spanks left, but I'm all for adding to the tally.

Ara does what I say, and the instant she's off my lap I glance at the wet spot on my leg. It's easily the size of my fist.

And I have huge hands.

I click the power button and start messing with the settings. "Ready for multiplayer mode, Kitty?"

CHAPTER 11

Ara

Oh. Em to the motherfucking G.

I lay back and obey Glitch and am immediately rewarded with, "Ready for multiplayer mode, Kitty?"

I don't know what he's going to do with my vibrator, but he exceeds expectations.

"Close your eyes," he rumbles softly.

Glitch is a goddamn unicorn. A demon unicorn. I'm still a little blissed out from the two orgasms I had on his lap—*I can't believe I did that*—and now here I am, at his mercy while he—

"Fuuuuck, *Glitch*." He runs my clit stimulator across my breasts, circling my nipples with the vibrator on the lowest setting. Without a word, he runs his hand up the back of my right calf, silently asking me to bend my legs. My thighs fall all the way open for him.

He pulls the vibrator away. "What happened to your knees?"

Huh? What knees?

I open my eyes and scramble to process what he asked. He's staring, brow deeply furrowed, concern etched in all his hardening features. "What happened here?"

Oh. "I fell."

He flicks his gaze to mine and cocks his brow again. God he's sexy. All disciplined and stern. "*Fell?*"

"Just before you got here. I ran and tripped and fell. Smashed my knees on the bathroom floor."

His features soften and he presses soft kisses to each of my kneecaps. Then I hear the vibrator click back on and I sigh with relief. He's the most attentive, observant, protective man I've ever met.

The vibrator touches my belly next and I second guess where to put my hands. I want to cover my belly but...

"You are so fucking sexy, Kitty."

My insecurity fades a little. Never mind that I just gave him a raunchy show and fingered myself on his lap. This is a whole different angle. One that makes me inventory every inch of my body. Glitch wouldn't say I'm sexy unless he really thought I was. So far, he's barely said anything.

Glitch runs the toy across my stomach, tickling me. Then he settles between my thighs, and I tense again.

"Relax," he says, placing a kiss on my inner thigh. "Enjoy it."

Oh, I'm enjoying it alright. But when he flicks his tongue out and licks my pussy, I'm not sure I have the capacity to relax. He shoves a finger inside me and hits that pad of flesh I sometimes have trouble finding myself. My toes curl. "Mmmph."

Glitch places the toy under his hand and starts flicking my clit with his tongue he uses the vibrator against my taint. He's... he's v-v-vibrating my —

My body seizes, the orgasm so strong and so fast, I don't have time to suck in air before I'm arching up and clawing my mattress. I swear I'm so dizzy I feel nauseous.

"Too fast." He hooks my thighs with his arms and holds me down. "Now I know better." He dives in again and I'm legit about to cry. I come a lot on my own, but I've never felt this intensity before. It's almost too much.

He places the vibrator on a different setting, making it pulse against my taint this time. If I move a little, it'll vibrate my asshole. Do I want that? I'm not even sure. And I don't have time to think more on it because Glitch is already back to business.

He plays with my body. Explores it. Switches tactics every time I'm getting close to coming again. I go from coming super-fast to being desperate for another. "Please," I say, drenched in sweat. "I need to come again."

Glitch ignores me and continues to lick and finger me in various ways. This man is methodical to a fault. I'm going to kill him if he doesn't let me come soon. I'm so desperate for it, I want to die. He works me up until I'm just at the edge, then backs off and switches tactics. He does this again, and again, and again.

I've never been edged before. I've tried to do it to myself, but I give in too easily. This is next level madness.

And it's fucking heaven.

"Please," I whimper, sinking my hands into his hair and shoving his mouth harder against my pussy. "*Please.*"

His eyes flick up and meet mine.

Then I get what I've begged for.

Glitch slams his finger against my g-spot, moves the toy until it's pulsating against my tightest hole, and he doesn't lick my clit. He fucking *feasts* on it.

I blow apart. My soul leaves my goddamn body. I scream until my vocal cords hurt and my cheeks tingle and I don't think I have limbs anymore. I keep careening in pleasure until I can't breathe.

Spots dot my vision. I'm going to faint.

I think I might stroke out.

The mattress shifts, and suddenly he's above me, his face is covered in my arousal. He smashes his mouth to mine in a brutal kiss, ripping another orgasm from my body with his hand and wet noises ring in my ears. "Holy shit," I rasp once he pulls away.

And then… I'm mortified.

Glitch is soaked. His face is glistening. His shirt is wet. When he pulls his fingers out of my pussy, his hand is drenched, too.

"What did I just do?"

"You relaxed… and enjoyed it." Glitch drags his diabolical tongue over his hand, from heel to fingertip. "Christ, Ara. You taste like sugar."

"It's the Skittles."

"Rainbows don't taste this amazing. Skittles aren't nearly this delicious."

I'm still blown away by the mess I've made. I squirted. I squirted all over him.

I've never done that before. I'm not sure what I'm supposed to do about it. "You're a mess."

He plucks at his shirt and looks down. "I still see dry spots."

"Holy fuck, Glitch." I cover my face with both hands. "I can't believe I just did that."

"You've never—"

"Drenched a lover before? No. Not even a tiny bit."

"*Lover?*"

Umm, what else do I call him? Boyfriend sounds lame. He feels like a bigger deal than that. Sex God comes to mind, Master too, but

Lover slipped out and now I'm unsure if he's insulted or amused.

He's kissing me again. I can taste myself on his mouth. It's confusing. Sexy. Glitch makes me feel safe, excited, and sensual at the same time. He's giving me a lot, but it feels like he's getting just as much, which, in my experience, is odd.

"You got anymore toys in there?" His question throws me off guard.

"Only a couple."

"Let me see."

I'm not sure why he wants them. I've come so much already, it's time to reciprocate. I sit and up reach for his belt buckle. Glitch grabs my wrist, his grip gentle, but firm. "Let me see the other toys, Kitty."

My cheeks burn. I empty my drawer, tossing the other three toys onto the bed—a glass dildo, a rabbit, and a wand.

He stares at them. Again, I can't read the expression on his face, but I know he's calculating. "This is all you have?"

Damnit. "You want everything, everything?"

He cocks his eyebrow, and I know I've just earned another spank. Flustered and flabbergasted, I roll off the bed and march out to the living room and grab my purse. I stomp back to him and toss a lipstick at his head.

Glitch is trying to keep his amusement hidden but fails once he pops off the lid to the lipstick and twists the bottom, making my compact travel companion buzz. "Wow."

"Wow good or wow bad?"

"Which is your favorite?"

"The one you just used on me."

"Which is your least favorite?"

I take a second to debate. "The glass dildo." It's curved and beaded, which I love the idea of. "I bought it a few months ago, but I've never used it."

His smile lights up the room. "Get back over here." He crooks his finger at me.

I obey, but I'm not sure I should. "When do I get a turn to have fun with you?"

"You aren't having fun with me now?"

"You know what I mean." I'm on my knees in front of him. He's fully dressed still. It's frustrating. "You haven't come at all yet."

He chuckles, and the rumbles hit me in the chest. Man, his voice is crazy deep.

"I've been fantasizing about you for a long time, Kitty. You're not the only one having fun doing this. You're absolutely incredible."

My brow furrows when he says that.

"You trust me," he explains. "You're giving me full access and—" Glitch shakes his head as he looks at my toys. "I just want to learn everything I can, so I know how to play the next round."

He's learning my body. My likes and dislikes. What makes me detonate.

I think I'm struggling to grasp this concept because no one's ever bothered to be thorough and generous with me before.

He takes the glass dildo out of its satin-lined box and examines it. This thing has a good weight to it, but it's slimmer than most dildos and about seven inches long. "Lay back," he orders.

I do as I'm told.

Glitch crawls on top of me and kisses me again as a reward. His tongue sweeps over mine and I swear I've never been kissed like this in my life. It's like we've done this a million times, but it's also new and exciting. He tastes amazing, and I know part of it is my cum. "Take your shirt off," I say, already dragging my nails up his ribcage under the fabric.

He sits back, reaches behind him, and pulls the t-shirt over his head.

Holy motherfucking fantasies. Glitch is stacked. I barely have time to look before he comes in for more of my mouth. "Heyyyy, Kitty," he growls against my lips. "You ready to purr for me again?"

I giggle. I fucking *giggle*.

This is the most fun I've had in my entire life.

How did it take this long for us to get together? Why didn't I try to connect with him sooner? How did I waste time with Jason when I could have been enjoying life with Glitch?

He nuzzles my neck while I'm overthinking, which means he can't read my expressions and I'm quick to compose them. I don't want to think about ex douchebags or anything other than—

"Glitch," I whimper when he shoves the dildo inside my pussy.

Jason would never let me use my toys when we were together. He was offended I needed them. But if I don't get a lot of stimulation at once, I can't come. And I never got enough of anything from Jason. Glitch is the exact opposite. If I like something, he seems to want to learn how to use it just to make me like it even more.

After a few pumps in my pussy, he pulls it out and shoves it into his mouth.

I… I… Good God, is that hot.

Glitch pulls the dildo out from between his lips, nice and slow, one beaded ridge at a time, until he's sucked the damned thing clean. "Fuck, Ara. You're so wet."

Annnnd I've just gotten wetter.

He spreads my legs apart and I see him glance at one of my scraped knees. "Does it hurt to bend your legs?"

"Nope."

He nods as if reconfirming it's okay for him to continue. Then his demeanor changes back to hungry Glitch with a meal in front of him.

As far as dinner dates go, I've never had better. I love being the meal.

He presses his thumb to my clit, applying just enough pressure to make me hold my breath, then he pushes the dildo back inside my pussy. He twists it, and since it's curved, I see stars again.

"Holy shit," I groan.

His muscles flex with every controlled breath he takes. "Look at me, Kitty."

I do and I am not ready for what he does next.

"Breathe," he says. Keeping constant pressure on my clit with his thumb, Glitch stimulates it while pulling the glass toy out of my pussy and then moving it to my ass.

I tense up when he starts to push it into my tight hole.

"Relax." He grins. "And enjoy."

I'm not sure what I'm expecting, but it's not this. The sensation is… incredible. The toy's so slick from my arousal that it glides in easily. "Holy shhhhhiiiit." My head drops back on the pillow, and I turn off every thought that's trying to ruin this moment.

It feels amazing and confusing.

Glitch applies a little more pressure to my clit and starts moving the toy in and out. I feel everything. My body burns. Tightens. Floats. "I'm gonna die," I moan.

"Want me to stop?"

"No," I rush to say. "Please no."

"Since you used such nice manners…" Glitch picks up speed on my clit and slows down on my ass.

I've never done any backdoor play before. This is insane.

"Oh my God, oh my God… Oh…. Myyyyy…." This next orgasm blasts out of me and feels entirely different. I lock down, my body squeezing and clamping on the toy as I scream while coming hard enough to see stars.

"Too fast," he says again.

I know what he's going to do before it happens.

I just hope I'm able to survive another edging.

CHAPTER 12

Glitch

Ara is a Goddess. A fiery, wicked deity I plan to stay on my knees for until this floating rock we're on blows to smithereens. I'm never going to get tired of making her come. The scent, the taste, the sounds. She's a full-bodied experience I wasn't prepared for.

I'm so grateful Trey found a way to shove us together. I'm forever in his debt.

I edge my girl for another half hour, playing with her body, learning and memorizing every inch. She's sweating and panting and flushed. I want to shove my cock inside her. Feel what it's like when her body grips my dick while she comes.

But that's not happening tonight. I want her to come back for more tomorrow. And the next day. And the next.

I'm marrying this woman, mark my words.

So my cock will stay where it is. Tonight is all about Ara.

I've never felt a connection like this with someone before. And for Ara to trust me wholeheartedly with her body is a gift I'll treasure until my last breath. We've wasted time tiptoeing around each other online, and I'm done with the distance and general convos. I want to know everything. Be part of everything.

Somewhere in the room, I swear I hear a little clicking noise. I look down and see the toys have rolled together on the mattress by my left leg. My little Kitty likes to play a lot. Good for her. And that travel-sized lipstick toy has my imagination on full blast.

I fuck her slowly with the glass dildo, adjusting the pressure on her clit with my thumb until I eventually lean in and replace it with my tongue. Then I shove two fingers in her pussy and stretch her a little more.

Three stimulants at once, and my multitasking skills are rewarded in under a minute.

Ara's screaming. Her body quakes under my hands. When she orgasms, I swear I feel just as good as she does. I'm not even joking. She's a mess under me. I've made her squirt, cream, laugh, and even cry with how overstimulated she is.

What a masterpiece.

I pull the dildo out and say, "Don't move." Then I get up and carefully place the toy in her bathroom for later.

Coming back, I'm not surprised she's moved. *Four*. Four more beautiful handprints are going on that luscious, bratty ass of hers.

She's staring at me, heavy-lidded and exhausted. Her hair is stuck to her sweet face. She's radiant, and I take immense pride knowing I helped get her this way.

"Do I get to suck your dick now?"

My eyebrows lift to my hairline. If she's not passed out, I haven't done my job well enough. "Do you want to?"

"Mmm hmm." But she's already closed her eyes. I quietly lay down beside my girl and spoon her until she falls asleep, which doesn't take long. Once I know she's knocked out, I creep out of the room and notice her cell buzzing in her purse. Whoever it is will have to wait. Hope it's not an emergency.

Speaking of which, I pull my cell out and check it. Beetle's called twice, but it's definitely past his bedtime, so I can't call back. He was probably bored out of his mind. He's grounded for getting that infraction, because yes, Erin found out about it. The principal called and told her. I feel bad he's having trouble in school, and I want to help him rebuild his make-believe world, but I'm secretly grateful he's lost gaming privileges for a week. It gives me undivided Ara time.

My stomach rumbles, and I glance at the clock. Holy shit, it's almost two am.

Time flies when you're having fun.

I pad quietly into her kitchen and put away the rest of the groceries we'd abandoned. Then I make myself useful for a little while. By the time I'm pulling pizza out of the oven, Ara's blinking sleepily at me from the doorway. "What are you doing?"

"Making dinner," I say with an easy smile. She's so perfect. Her hair's a knotty mess on her head, and she's put on little shorts and an anime t-shirt with the neckline cut big, so it falls off her shoulders. All she's missing is the tube socks.

"I thought you'd left." She looks confused.

I gently close her oven door and rest the pizza on her stovetop. "Do you want me to leave?" Not gonna lie, my heart's in my throat waiting for her answer.

"No, I just…"

"Thought I'd have my way with you and skip out once your guard's down."

Her silence is confirmation enough.

Jesus, she must have dated some real fuckheads to automatically think that of me. "I didn't stay so you'd suck me off, either." I fear that's where her head went next. "I honestly just wanted to stay and make dinner."

"At two am?"

I'm not sure what's happening here, or why the atmosphere between us has changed. "If you want me to leave, I can g—"

"No!" She cuts me off. "Ugh." Ara scrubs her face with both hands and groans. "I'm sorry. I'm fucking this up, aren't I?"

Yes and no. I'm not even sure. "This is a lot. I get it. And that's my fault." I cross my arms over my chest and lean against the counter.

Ara comes into the kitchen, her shoulders slumped. "I'm in my head again. It keeps happening."

She wasn't in her head back in the bedroom.

Or was she?

I suddenly realize Ara's an enigma I might never fully figure out. Maybe that's okay. Or maybe I need to give us more time. Probably both.

"I feel like I've known you forever," I say cautiously. "Is that weird?"

"No." She comes even closer. "I feel the same way. I just wasn't gonna say it."

"I should probably get going."

"But you made pizza."

"I figured you'd be hungry. And thirsty." I point at the glass of water with ice I'd left on the counter. I was going to bring her dinner in bed, but she woke before I was done setting things up. I think she figures that out when she sees the origami rose next to and the glass, both set on a cookie sheet because I wasn't sure what else to use as a tray to bring it all to her.

"You're taking care of me," she whispers. This is the second time Ara's referenced what I've done in a way that makes it sound like a phenomenon.

Her eyes sail to mine, and I see she's close to crying. Only instead of come-too-hard tears, these are more delicate. Vulnerable.

"Heyyyy." I close the space between us. Cupping her face, I swipe my thumb over her cheek to catch her first tear. "Why are you upset?"

"I'm not upset."

I feel like a piece of shit. I've gone overboard and shouldn't have. I just thought I'd read her right, and she wanted what I did, and now I'm afraid I've misunderstood the whole thing. "You look upset, Ara."

"I'm just so mad at myself for not asking for your number sooner."

Her confession shocks me.

"I can't tell you how many times I'd log onto Discord and go into our channel, Glitch. Then I'd chicken out on saying anything and close it."

"I was no better." The energy between us shifts a little. The tightness in my chest slightly eases. "I should have put myself out there a long fucking time ago, Ara." Instead, I kept my distance and nearly lost her when she started dating someone else.

"No more dragging our feet," she says. "Promise?"

"Sooo, we're getting married in an hour?"

Her laugh warms my body from tongue to toes. But I'm only half joking. I'd marry her on the spot, right here, right now, if it was possible. I know Ara's meant to be mine.

Her cell buzzes in the living room. She looks over, her brow furrowing.

"You gonna answer?" If someone was calling me this late, I'd be worried.

"No." Her tone is guarded.

Annnd now I'm on high alert. Does she already know who that would be, calling her so late? "Is there something going on I can help with?"

"No." But she's cagey again and I don't like it. "I've already handled it."

If that was true, she wouldn't be having this reaction to a middle-of-the-night phone call she won't answer. I bite my tongue because if she doesn't want me to know, that's her decision and I'll respect it.

"It's Jason," she says. "I'm almost sure of it. He does this sometimes. I've blocked him, but he uses other people's phones to call me from."

"Maybe you should check to be sure? What if it's a family member or something with an emergency?"

She gives me a long, solemn look, then pads over to the couch and digs her phone out. I turn and plate two slices of pizza, so I don't look like a rabid guard dog foaming at the mouth. Ara comes back in and takes her plate from me. "It was him."

Do not be aggressive. Do not be possessive.

"He always breathes heavy into the phone."

I'm glad I haven't picked my plate up yet because I'm sure it would break under my clenching hand. Taking in a few deep breaths, I hope I sound calm when I ask, "How long ago did you break up?"

"About six weeks ago. Just after he broke my computer."

"I'm glad you got away from that asshole."

"Me too."

I grab my plate and follow her out to the little dining table between the kitchen and living room. I glance at her door and immediately plan out a new security system for her apartment. One deadbolt doesn't cut it for me.

"Thank you for telling me," I say, sitting down across from her.

"Thanks for listening."

I'll always listen. I'm good at it, and I want her to know she can come to me about anything—something I wish she'd known sooner.

Ara shrugs. "He'll get over it."

I leave it alone, but I'm not convinced she's right. Ara's amazing and Jason's lost her. Even if it's his own fault, that doesn't mean he won't regret it enough to try and beg her for another chance. He's done that plenty of times already and his persistence has paid off in the past.

But I can't let that stop me from showing her there's better out there than that fuckface.

"Olives, huh?" I chomp down.

"Are you judging me, Glitch?"

"A little." I take another bite.

"Better than pineapple."

"I knew it." I lean back and wipe my mouth with a napkin. "I just *knew* there'd be something about you that wasn't perfect."

"Hey!" She laughs and takes another bite of her veggie-laden pizza. Her gaze narrows at me. "You seriously like pineapple on your pizza?"

Shrugging, I sip my water and sit back. "Is that a deal breaker?"

"Maybe." She's so cheeky.

After we banter back and forth and devour the entire pizza, Ara yawns and she grabs our plates to carry them back into the kitchen.

"I can wash."

"I've got it, Glitch. Just sit down for a second and relax." After cleaning our plates, she wipes her hands dry and comes back to the table. "What time does your shop open?"

"Eleven." It's four am at this point. "I don't have to go in, though." I never really do. My shop is a well-oiled machine that basically runs itself. I just go in because I like having control and seeing the kids enjoy themselves in the safe space I've created for them.

Ara twirls a tendril of her pink hair around her finger. "Do you want to see my studio?"

"Abso-fucking-lutely."

Her smile is massive. "Yay!" She grabs her purse from the couch.

"Wait, you mean *now*?"

CHAPTER 13

Ara

I'm elated Glitch is willing to go to my studio. Who cares if it's before the ass crack of dawn? That power nap I took gave me a second wind, and I'm ready for another round of anything with this man.

I have plenty of canvases, sketchbooks, and supplies at my apartment, but I want to show him what I do. How I do it. I want to give him a peek at the me that's not on my best behavior. The raw parts. The insecure parts. The real deal.

I rent space on the top floor of an old warehouse because it has the best light. When we pull up, the building is completely deserted and the streetlamp flickers by the front door. Glitch looks up and frowns. "You work here?"

"Yup." I know it doesn't look great from the outside, but it's the inside that counts.

"There's no security," he says as we head towards the door. "There's nothing and no one keeping you safe."

"It's fine." I unlock the door and give it a good shove to open it. "Really. No one comes in here who doesn't belong. And the place is usually packed with people."

"How many?"

"Five of us rent space here."

Glitch looks at me like five isn't a huge number and certainly wouldn't be his definition of "packed." I don't blame him. We've never had a safety issue here before, but that doesn't mean it can't happen.

"The guy on the first floor is a sculptor. He has two dogs he takes with him everywhere he goes. They usually run the hallway on the main floor, and no one can even walk by the building without them barking their asses off." Which has led to arguments because the dogs are great for guarding but shit for concentration.

I head towards the steps, and Glitch follows. "The elevator's broke. These steps are my only form of exercise most days." We climb the stairwell and Glitch looks more and more concerned by the time we reach my floor. I want to be annoyed, but I'm not. He's only thinking about my safety, and I love that. It's nice to be worried about.

I unlock the door to my studio and the smell of acrylics and wood smacks us in the face. I flick on the lights and smile big. "Welcome to where the magic happens." Okay, that sounded cooler in my head.

Glitch blinks up at the light fixtures first.

"They're full-spectrum fluorescents," I say because now my geek is showing. Even with a full wall of windows, I wanted fixed light because the colors can shift from warm to cool depending on the time of day and what lights you use. Besides, I'm here most nights well after sundown. Glitch slowly takes in everything from floor to ceiling, walking leisurely around the room while I watch him. I notice he keeps his hands clasped behind his back, as if he's afraid to touch anything in here.

He stops at a stack of canvases I have in the corner. Looking back at me, he points to the stack. "May I?"

"Absolutely." I love that he asked permission before rummaging through my things. I've never let anyone come here before. This is my private space. More private than my apartment in terms of where my soul lives. I'm not sure if I'd have liked it if Glitch just helped himself. But now that he's asked, I add, "You can look at anything. Everything." I want to be an open door for him. I want Glitch to *want* to look inside and see who I am.

Bringing him here is the best way to share myself.

"This is incredible, Ara." His voice is deeper than normal. And softer.

"That's my 'not quite good enough' pile."

He cocks his brow at me. Every time he's made that expression, it's earned me a spanking.

Does me saying my art isn't good enough mean I get in trouble?

"Why do you think these aren't good enough?"

"Lots of reasons." I saunter over. "They just don't hit right yet. Sometimes I can figure out what's missing and make it better, but a lot of times, I stare at them and imagine setting them on fire. It's a love-hate thing."

Glitch carefully flips through the various sized canvases. He stops at the second to last one. His breath catches. "Fuck, Ara." He plucks it out and brings it up to the front of the pile and steps back to appreciate it better.

I instantly swell with pride. It doesn't matter that I hate this particular painting. It doesn't matter that I found a million flaws in my body with my self-portrait. In this pose, I'm naked, sitting on the floor with one hand stretched up, fingers curled, eyes darting to the side. I sat this way because it made me feel impish and goddess-like, which I loved. But my inner feelings didn't translate as well as I'd intended.

Glitch swallows as he takes it all in. Heat rolls off him and slams into me. "I want this."

Umm. "It's not finished."

"I can't imagine what you think needs improvement. It's fucking stunning, Ara."

Nice of him to say, but I disagree. "It's got a lot wrong with it."

"No." He pivots to face me, his gaze hot as fire. "It's breathtaking. You're... fuck, you're perfect."

I was also skinnier in this picture and now I'm starting to squirm. Did he notice the weight difference between this painting and what I looked like on my bed earlier?

"Who took this photo?"

His question throws me off. "I set up my tripod and snap pictures or take video, then I freeze the frame and work off it." It's something I'm still getting used to. "I keep trying to find ways to love my body." Clearly, I failed.

"What's not to love?"

I don't even answer that. "I'm better with the images in my head." I lure him over to another stack of canvases. "See?"

He cards through them gently. "Wow."

My smile hurts, it's so big. I swear the two of us have smiled more at each other tonight than I have, collectively, over the past five years.

"I bow down to your talent, Ara. I don't have an artistic bone in my body."

"I'm sure that's not true."

"Oh it is, I assure you."

"Then who painted your shop?" Because now I know it wasn't him.

"A senior from the high school did it about two years ago. It was for his portfolio."

"And you let him use your shop?"

Glitch shrugs. "He needed it, I had it, and I admire what he did. I'll never paint over it."

I didn't think I could possibly love him more, but there he goes proving me wrong. "You're pretty amazing, you know that?"

He turns his dark green eyes on me. "So are you."

Glitch makes me feel like I could fly. How the hell is it possible to feel this confident and solid with someone I barely know? "Can I..." *Oh boy, here goes nothing.* "Can I paint you?"

The look on his face is priceless. "Yeah. I'd love that."

"Yay!" I start tugging on the hem of his shirt. "Take this off."

"You want to paint me *now*?"

"When inspiration strikes," I chirp, sashaying my hips, walking backwards to grab a blank canvas. "You gotta be ready to ride it."

He laughs and pulls his shirt off. "I'm not sure if you're talking about your muse or me."

"Both." I wink and snatch my graphite set.

Glitch rubs the back of his neck, looking around. "Where should I stand?"

"Get naked first."

His eyes widen. "So we're going nude." Then he barks a laugh. "Okay. I'm game."

I can tell he's nervous, but he's being an amazing sport about this. "Lean against the wall. One hand up behind your head, the other relaxed by your side."

He kicks off his shoes and unbuckles his belt. In total silence, Glitch gives me everything I'm asking of him. I sit on the floor while he gets in the pose I want, and he looks awkward and adorable. Then he pretends to toss his hair back and says, "Draw me like one of your French girls."

I rock back on the floor, laughing so hard. I've never felt this excited and peaceful at the same time before. Within a half-hour, I've roughly sketched the masterpiece that is Glitch. "You want to see it?"

"You're done already?"

"For now." With the great conversations we've been having, time flew by. Plus, I'm a fast sketcher when I have a great model.

"Tada!" I spin it around and Glitch's eyes widen. "You like?" It's rough but won't stay that way. I have a plan for this masterpiece.

"You only drew my face."

"I know." My wicked ways are devious and genius.

"I thought you were drawing my whole body." He laughs, gesturing at his nakedness.

"Oh." I jab a finger towards the larger canvases. "You want me to get one of the three-by-six canvases out and draw you an actual true-to-size dick pic?"

Glitch's burst of laughter rocks the entire room. His head is thrown back, his abs contracting, and his hard-on bounces as he keeps laughing. "God, I fucking love you."

My breath catches. I know it's just a saying, but it didn't feel innocent. It felt true. And I find myself crawling across the floor of my studio to get to him. I stop by his feet and stare up at the most perfect man I've ever met, and I can't believe this night has been so damn magical. And then it gets even better.

Glitch cups the side of my cheek and says, "Heyyy, Kitty."

I want to suck him off so bad, I almost beg for it.

CHAPTER 14

Glitch

This date keeps elevating, and I don't want it to ever stop. As I stare down at Ara looking up at me like a little cat, I'm spiraling. I want to fuck her mouth. I want to fuck her pussy. I want to slam her against the window and fuck her in the ass. I want to eat her cunt and dump paint all over her body just to run my fingers through a rainbow of colors on her sweet skin.

I'm not leaving this studio without that painting of her I found earlier.

Hell, I'm not leaving this studio without making it clear that she's mine. Today. Tomorrow. Forever.

The sun's starting to rise and the rays creep into her studio. With my hand on her cheek, I guide her mouth to my length.

"Put that pretty, hot little mouth on me, Kitty."

She opens eagerly and licks the ridge of my head. I lose my breath. Ara delivers more than my expectations can handle. She rises onto her knees and sucks me down until I hit the back of her throat. I'm not even halfway in, and I swear I see stars. She sucks me hard, and the hollows of her cheeks are defined as she pulls back.

Holy fucking shit. Ara could likely suck my soul right out of my dick with her level of enthusiasm.

I grab the back of her head and guide her down my length again. I pull back to let her twirl her tongue around my head before I thrust forward to fuck her mouth a little more. "You feel so good, Kitty." My register is damn deep while I talk. "My dirty little artist has a mouth made to suck my cock."

She lets out a little groan. It zings through my balls.

"Fuck, Ara, that's it. Take me down. A little more, that's it." I rock into her mouth slowly as she slurps at me. That sound will be my kryptonite. "Stroke it." With both my hands threaded in her hair at this point, I fuck her pretty mouth until I can't breathe. She's so good, so perfect, so wild on her knees, using one hand to stroke my base while twirling and sucking my head, her other hand grips around my damn balls, massaging and tugging and squeezing.

"Such a good girl, making me feel this good." I'm close. So close. "I want you to swallow me, Kitty. Take everything I'm gonna give you. Don't waste a fucking drop."

She picks up pace and sucks harder.

"That's it, Kitty."

Her eyelashes flutter and have clumped together. She stares up at me with my dick in her mouth and tears clinging to her long eyelashes and there's fire in her eyes.

"Awww fuuuuuck." My balls draw up, the hair on the back of my neck stands on end. I climax like a storm unleashed. I'm trapped at her mercy as I unload down her throat. I can't move. My thighs flex, my shoulders slam the wall, and she leans forward, desperate to take as much of me down her throat as she can. My cock pulses and I keep coming. Even after I think it's over, she doesn't let up. Ara swirls her tongue around my sensitive tip and sucks me back down again.

A deep, guttural growl tears out of my throat.

My fingers in her hair tighten as she gently sucks the head, doing all kinds of sinful things with her tongue and before I know it, I'm about to come a second time. I pull out and start to jack off. "Open your mouth and hold out your tongue."

She does as I say, and I spurt my cum all over her pretty pink tongue, chin, and the top of her tits. Her t-shirt is hanging off her shoulder and I want to cut the whole damn thing off so I can paint her body with what's pumping out of me.

"Holy fuck," I rasp. I can't seem to stop. It's like my body's been waiting for this moment for forever and if I take a break, the magic will die. I refuse to let that happen.

Dropping down on my knees, I gently push Ara onto her back as I kiss her. She tastes salty and sweet, and I know it's me on her tongue and I fucking love the way we taste together.

"Mmmph." She pushes against me, and I back off a little. Before I ask if I'm going too hard, she swipes her fingers across the top of her tits and gathers my cum, then she shoves all four of her fingers in her mouth at once and sucks them clean.

Fuck me sideways, that's hot.

"You like the taste of my cream, Kitty?"

"Yes," she moans.

I pull down her cotton shorts. "You want more?"

Her eyes widen. She looks between us and sees I'm still fully hard. "You're a machine," she whispers.

"I'm a hungry animal." I bend down and show her just how starved I am for her sweet pussy. Shoving two fingers into her sopping wet cunt, I lean down and suck her clit in earnest, making her come within seconds. *Seconds*. She didn't even last a minute under my touch this time, and I'm dying to see how many orgasms it'll take for her to pass out again.

"Glitch!" She slams her thighs around my head, and I rise from on my knees, my mouth still latched onto her clit. Her ass and back lift off the floor in this position. "GLITCH!" She comes with only my tongue on her this time. "Holy shit, my head's spinning."

I bet it is.

I nearly have her tipped upside down. Once I'm sure she's finished pulsing around my finger, I slowly ease Ara back down until she's lying flat on the floor again and I drag my tongue along her slick folds. "You ready for another?"

"*Another*?" She can't catch her breath. "I'm gonna die if you give me another."

"RIP you, then." I descend on her pussy and have her screaming my name in less than thirty seconds. For all the edging I gave Ara in her apartment, I'm not even trying to be patient in her studio. I just want her coming. I want to keep hearing her scream my name. I want to make her hear colors.

She braces her feet against my shoulders and shoves away.

I allow it so she can catch her breath again. But not for long. "Where are you going, Kitty?"

She crab-crawls away and I slink after her on my hands and knees. It's a slow stalking. A leisurely prowl. When Ara's back hits the window, she smiles at me.

"My girl wants it against the glass?" Then she'll have it against the glass. I'll build a shuttle and fucking take her to the moon if she asks me to. Anything for my Ara. "Stand up," I order.

Her sweaty skin skids up the windowpane, making it squeak a little as she does what she's told. I gently grab her ankle and place it on my shoulder as I stare up at her. This woman is a masterpiece. Soft curves, swollen lips, wicked eyes, knotted hair, flushed skin. I kiss the sore spot on her knee before I glance up at her again. "You're mine, Ara."

She bites her bottom lip. Little wrinkles form between her brows.

"Say it. Say you're fucking mine." I flick my tongue out and drag it along the seam of her pussy. "Mine."

"Yes." She sinks her hand into my hair. "I'm yours."

"That's right, Kitty. We belong to each other now. No one's making you come but me." Something odd flitters across her face. "Say what's in your head, Ara." Because I plan to make her non-verbal before I'm done on my knees.

"I come a lot," she confesses.

Interesting choice of words. "Is that a problem?"

"Is it?" she shoots back. "I mean, I come *a lot*, Glitch. I need it. It's like a compulsion."

Be still my Ara-owned heart. "You like to pleasure yourself often?"

"Mmm hmm."

"Nothing wrong with that."

Her cheeks turn a deeper crimson. "But you said—"

"I didn't mean you couldn't touch yourself, Kitty." I shove a finger inside her, loving how her inner walls grip me. "But I don't want another man touching you."

She lets out a little exhale that sounds like relief and it makes me wonder if her ex told her self-love was wrong. Some douchebags have a problem with that, but that's their insecurity talking. And I'm willing to bet my next paycheck that her ex also had a problem with the toys she used.

"Do you get off here in the studio?" I add another finger to her pleasure points.

"Mmm hmm." Her gaze is hooded, but she maintains eye contact with me.

"You use your lipstick toy?"

"Or…" Her grip tightens on my hair as I continue to finger her. "Or my hands."

"Right here on the floor?"

"And against this window."

The image of my Kitty getting herself off in the middle of all this paint with the fluorescent lights shining down on her like a motherfucking spotlight is something I need to see. "Show me." I pull out and hold her steady until she's got both feet on the floor again. "Show me what you do to yourself, Ara."

I make sure my tone and expression both show how very eager I am to watch.

"But I—"

My eyebrow lifts. She pauses, knowing that's another spank she's just earned. "Show me what you do, Kitty. Tell me what you think about while you do it."

With no shorts on, and her t-shirt still hanging over her shoulder, Ara saunters to the center of the room and sits on the floor. Pulling her shirt off, she crumples it up and makes a pillow with it. Then my beautiful girl lies back and spreads her legs, giving me the best art show of my life.

Her toes curl as she dips two fingers inside the pussy that now belongs to me. Then she rubs those slickened fingers in tight circles over her clit, alternating between fast and slow, then she dips them into her pussy again and starts the process over.

"Does that feel good?"

"You feel better." She groans, her eyes still shut. "Mmph." She picks up the pace, rubbing her clit with three fingers now. Her legs are spread wide, baring everything to me. I want to partake. No, fuck that, I want to take over. But I don't.

"Talk to me, Kitty. What are you thinking about?"

"You fucking me." Her pussy's so wet, it's getting noisy, and it makes my mouth water.

"Where am I fucking you, Kitty?" I crawl closer to her. My cock's throbbing, aching to sink into her heat.

She starts panting. "You… you fuck me everywhere. You're in my mouth… my cunt…" Her thighs begin to shake. "You fuck my ass…" Her toes curl, feet flex and her ass goes in the air as her back arches. She screams. I'm talking a full-blown, throat wide, thunderstruck roar rips from her throat as she orgasms.

My wild beauty squirts all over the floor and continues to rub another out as I make my way closer.

Ara's still catching her breath when I crawl on top of her. "Such a good, messy girl." I capture her mouth with mine and dominate the kiss. I want to feed her my cock again and I want to make all her desires reality. I'll fuck her wherever, however, whenever she wants. I'm hers to command.

"Ara?" someone yells from the other side of the door. "Are you okay?"

Her eyes flip open. Dogs bark in the hall. She holds her face and whispers, "*Shit*."

"Ara?"

"I'm fine!"

"Okay, just checking." There's some shuffling behind the door and a dog yips. "I have some bagels if you want one."

"No thank you!"

"Suit yourself."

We stay dead quiet as we listen to the dude with his bagels and two dogs leave again. I'm secretly torn between grateful and angry for that fucker. On one hand, he checked on Ara and was concerned for her safety, which I like. On the other, he got to hear her come, which I hate.

"I'm not usually loud," she whispers. "I can't seem to keep quiet with you, though."

Not gonna lie, my pride just puffed out. I kiss her again and she's all kinds of worked up under my hands. I want to fuck her on the floor but won't. "I want you so much it hurts. But I don't want to share even the sound of your climax with someone else." If that makes me an asshole, oh well. It's the truth. "Can you keep quiet?"

Ara swallows hard and looks down at my eager cock. It's so hard and veiny, it's got its own pulse.

"No," she whispers. "I don't want to have to hold back. Not during our first time."

"Then let's get out of here."

She takes my hand and I haul her to her feet. "Where are we going? Back to my place?"

"Nope." I pick up her clothing and help her get dressed. "We're going to mine."

CHAPTER 15

Ara

Glitch is a unicorn demon. Have I said that already? Probably, but it bears repeating. This man is a wet dream come true, and I'm going to bind myself to him for life. I've never given marriage much thought before. I'm hardly thinking of it now. If that's not something he wants, I won't press it. I just want him. Forever. I don't need to sign some contract for that to happen.

But I will sell my soul to the devil to make it last an eternity.

He drives my car back to his place and keeps his hands on my thigh the whole way. It's a little possessive and calming at the same time. I feel like a live wire that's been zapping for hours. When will it fizzle out?

I have a feeling the answer's *never* as long as Glitch is around.

We pull into a cul-de-sac that's all townhouses. I'm not sure what I was expecting, but this surprises me a bit. "You live alone?"

"Yeah." He opens the garage door and drives in. Cutting the engine, he gets out and opens the passenger door for me. I'm grateful because my limbs are heavy. My body's spent. Glitch guides me inside his home and flicks on the lights.

It smells amazing in here. Like lemons and clean laundry. And it's immaculate. Glitch drops my key fob on his breakfast bar and grabs my hand. There's a lot going on—electronics, artwork, books. "You read?" I pluck the first novel I see and glance at the title. It's a vampire romance.

"Love to when I've got the time."

"You read *romance* novels?" I can't believe it. Why can't I believe it? I should. The man is a fucking devil on my body, he must have learned these tricks from somewhere.

"I do more than read them." He tugs me along. "Come here."

I follow Glitch into his bedroom and towards a closet.

Oh, here it is. The moment the bubble will pop.

If he opens that closet door and puts me in some kind of cage because he's a serial killer, I'll be so damn mad. Instead of chains and a dog bowl dish for his captives, I find one hell of a recording setup—complete with soundproof pads on the walls and ceiling. "Whoa. You turned your walk-in closet into a recording studio?"

Glitch shrugs. "It's a side hustle. Trey talked me into it. Said my voice was perfect for audiobooks, and since he knows a lot of authors, he was able to help me get a foothold in the business."

I can't even believe this. "You narrate audiobooks."

"Smutty ones, mostly."

My eyebrows lift to my hairline. "I want to listen to one."

"I was hoping you'd say that." He pulls out his chair and taps the seat. "Put your sweet ass right here." As I do, he grabs a set of headphones and places them on my ears. His monitor lights up and he starts clicking various files and hits *play* on one of clips.

His voice hits my ears with a deep, raspy, *"Heyyyy, Kitty."*

My thighs clench. My pulse races.

"Why don't you crawl over here? That's it. Nice and slow." I glance up at Glitch. This is what audiobooks are like? How have I never listened to one before?

"Did you miss this cock?"

I stare at his crotch and see he's hard. Leaning against the desk, arms crossed over his chest, Glitch smiles down at me.

"Open your mouth so I can give you a gift."

I pull the headphones off. "Someone wrote this in a book?"

Because. Take. My. Money.

"I wrote that," he confesses.

It's a good thing I'm sitting down because otherwise my knees might have buckled.

"I wrote that and a lot more." He hits the computer keys again. "See?"

I glance at the screen. The folder is titled Kitty Series and there are a ton of tracks.

Glitch massages the back of his neck and looks a little uncomfortable. "You showed me your works that are still in progress. Thought I could share mine with you too."

I hold the headphones up to my ears again, hit play on another track, and listen to his dirty words. It makes me break out in a sweat.

He shuts off the recording. "They're about you."

All oxygen evacuates my lungs. *They're about you.*

He pulls the headphones off.

They're about you.

"I've been in love with you for a long time, Ara. Even if that doesn't seem possible or sound true, it is. I've fantasized about you so often, I needed to channel it somehow because I didn't think this," he says, waving his hand between us, "was ever going to happen."

I can't swallow. My throat's too tight. "You call me Kitty."

He calls me Kitty. Holy shit. I look at the files in the folder and try to count how many there are. He's recorded dozens and dozens of dirty talking ear porn about me for months. I'm equally flattered, turned on, and super confused. "But you didn't ever talk to me," I whisper. "Even in Discord, you kept our conversations so general."

"A mistake I'll regret for the rest of my life."

I believe him. I wish Glitch had acted sooner. Shit, I wish *I* had acted sooner. I should have thrown myself out there but didn't. I let my insecurities get in my way and keep me from going after what I wanted most.

This man.

I wish there was a way I could plug a wire between us and download everything about him. "What's your real name?"

"Sean."

My favorite name. I'm so not saying that out loud, because he'd probably never believe me, but Sean is my most favorite guy name in the world. What are the odds? "How did you get the name Glitch?"

"My sister gave me that when I was a kid. Every time I got too nervous or worked up about something, my brain would short-circuit. I couldn't speak or think straight. She'd say I was glitching, and it stuck."

I love it. "Can I meet her someday?"

"You can meet her today, if you want."

Are we moving too fast? Or are we not moving fast enough? I can't figure my shit out and anxiety starts to bubble in my belly.

Glitch sees it happen and acts fast. "Hey. Whoa."

I don't know why I'm freaking. I don't know why I'm tearing up.

"Ara, look at me."

He's blurry because I'm about to cry.

Glitch cups my face and kisses my forehead. "We've got all the time in the world, Kitty. We don't have to rush anything. You can meet her some other time. We dragged our feet, but we still made it to each other. I meant what I said in your studio. You're mine."

Annnd now I'm really crying. This is pathetic.

"Is that bad? Did I say something wrong?" He tilts my face so I'll look at him. "Talk to me, Ara."

I feel horrible already for what I'm about to say. "If I hadn't been so stupid, I would have had you longer." And not ever had to experience the nightmare of my last boyfriend. But I can't say that part out loud. I don't want Glitch to know how awful Jason was. I don't want to ruin this new, shiny relationship with the ugliness of that jerk.

"Never call yourself stupid again, understand?"

I don't react.

"Ara." He dips his face to mine and holds my stare. "*Never* call yourself that again."

I nod because I'm not sure I can speak. My mind is swarming with a million thoughts at once, and all of them are awful.

You're lucky you found someone who's willing to date you, Ara.

You're so pathetic.

You call this art? A pig would be a better model than you. Look at yourself. You're lucky I can see past your flaws. Who did you paint those nudes for, Ara? Your gaming buddies?

Why can't you keep your hands off yourself? You're a filthy fucking whore. A pig whore. You're disgusting. It's a good thing I love you because no one else will.

I see Glitch's mouth move, but I'm not able to connect the words or process them because all I hear are the mean, awful things my exes have said about me. And Jason's horrible voice makes my blood freeze when I remember him saying, *"You only ever go online to be with those losers because you're too stupid for real conversation. Those paint fumes go to your head, Ara? Be glad I have a real job so we can still go out and afford dinner when all you do is play with your paint all day. Maybe you should suck my dick to show how you appreciate having a real man."*

Suddenly, Glitch is smashing his mouth to mine. His smell, his taste, his touch, his control over me vanquishes every bad thought from my brain. Burns them with the heat of his desire and I'm left floating in the chair, breathless.

He eases back, worry forcing his brows to dig down. "What just happened?"

I don't want to explain it. I don't want to say. But I promised myself to not hold back with Glitch, and so far, so good. "I have a lot of insecurity."

He doesn't react. At. All.

"I've dated a lot of shitbags"

Still no reaction.

"I sometimes can't keep their nasty words out of my head. It makes me panic or freeze, and I'm trying to not let them in because I don't want to ruin what we have going, so I just freaked out a little bit and I swear I'll do better. I just need a minute to reconfigure."

I just need a minute to *reconfigure*? What the fuck am I, a computer program? Oh my God, I want to crawl under a rock now.

Glitch has yet to move.

"Say something," I whisper.

His jaw clenches. The tendons in his neck become more defined. He stares and stares and stares at me. His voice trembles when he asks, "Which one?"

"W-which one what?"

"Which sorry ass, piece of shit do you want me to kill first?"

I let out a small, exasperated laugh.

"I'm not joking, Ara." He blindly reaches behind him and snatches a pad of paper and a pen and slams them on the desk. "Names, addresses, places of business."

"Glitch."

"Ara."

"Glitch!" I smack my hand on the notepad. "It's not funny!"

"And I'm not laughing." He keeps his tone calm, but I can see in his eyes he's close to boiling over. "You just fritzed out because you're haunted by the hateful words of men who didn't deserve you, and you expect me to not address it?"

I'm not sure what to say. "You can't just go after them."

"The hell I can't." He spins my chair and plants his hands on the armrests. "I'm so fucking sorry. I'm sorry I took so long to get to you. I'm sorry you had to ever be around an asshole who couldn't appreciate what he had. I'm sorry you don't see your beauty like I do, or that you can't grasp how truly insanely amazing you are." He jerks the chair, making my heart leap in surprise. "I'll spend all day, every day, telling you the truth. I'll growl them in your ear, carve them into your dreams. You're the most beautiful creature I've ever met. You're funny and talented and built like a goddamn wet dream."

I start to cry again.

Glitch cups my face and wipes away my tears. "You're witty and sweet and silly." He kisses me tenderly. "You drive me wild with your laugh, did you know that? I'm gonna have hearing damage from how loud I turn up the volume whenever we play online. I can't get enough of your laugh. Your voice." He kisses me some more. "The way you hand Carson and Trey their own asses." He kisses down my neck. "The way you make me hard when all you do is type 'Hi' to me on Discord."

He lifts the hem of my shirt and pulls it off me. "I dream about you every night. Have for over a year." Glitch lifts me off the chair and I end up bracing my hands against his desk while he pulls my shorts down. "I've jacked off to the image of you every day for months."

My nipples harden instantly.

"Do you like knowing that, Kitty?"

I do. I really, really fucking do.

"Answer me."

"Y-yes."

"I imagined what you'd look like. I tried to find you online and couldn't."

I swallow through the tightness in my throat. "And… now that you've seen me?"

Glitch wraps my pink hair around his fist and bends my head back a little. "My imagination did *not* do you justice, Ara. Not by a fucking longshot."

I want to say he's making it up to make me feel better, but his hard cock shuts me up because erections don't lie. He presses his length against my ass cheeks and says, "I want that fucking painting of you. A want a house filled with paintings of you."

I hear his buckle release and the whooshing sound of his jeans dropping. Glitch stands behind me, getting naked while I'm reeling with his confessions.

"I can't stand the idea of someone else getting a glimpse of your magnificent body." He palms my tits, roughly, tentatively. When he pinches my nipples, I cry out. "And if you gain weight, lose weight, dye your hair, shave your head, or change in anyway, I want a portrait of it. I want all of you. All your phases, all your transitions." He bites down on my shoulder, making my toes curl. "I want to see your belly round with my baby. I want to kiss your stretch marks. I want to take care of you when you're exhausted and even when you're full of energy and life. I want to pop into your studio whenever I want and watch you be deadlocked on your paintings, so lost with your muse you can't even see me standing there admiring what you are and what you create."

"God, Glitch." He's making my heart unfurl.

"I want you to come to me for anything you need." He lets go of my hair and grips my waist. "And I want you to always be able to handle yourself with confidence." He spits into his hand and rubs it along the head of his dick. I'm slick enough already, but knowing he just did that makes me even more needy for him.

"You're mine, Ara. And I *always* take care of what's mine." He spreads my ass cheeks and I bend over to give him better access to my pussy.

I clench my hands and hold my breath. He means every word he says. If I've learned one thing about Glitch, it's that he doesn't waste his goddamn breath. Not even online when we're playing games.

This isn't a game.

This is real.

Glitch is mine.

He leans forward and growls against me, "I hope your muse is prepared, Kitty." And before I can ask what that's supposed to mean, he hits a button on his computer and the entire walk-in closet fills with this sound of his deep, dirty voice talking to me.

"Heyyyy, Kitty."

CHAPTER 16

Glitch

I never knew I was half-beast until tonight. With Ara in my space, her tears in my hands, and her body bent over my desk, I'm fucking feral for her.

Smashing the play button, Ara's going to hear every recording I've ever made for her. Every depraved word. All my fantasies I've conjured so far. *"Heyyyy, Kitty."*

While she listens to my dirty words, I rub the tip of my dick against her pussy.

What I wouldn't give to push my way in and fill her, stretch her, claim her.

"Touch yourself for me." My recorded voice is damn deep. The bass rumbles my chest as it plays through the speakers.

Ara slips her hand between herself and the desk. I smile. She's so wonderfully obedient sometimes.

"Just like that. Be a good little slut and rub your clit. That's it. Mmm, just like that. Go faster. Harder. Ffffuck, keep going." My recorded voice sucks in a harsh breath. *"Now stop."*

Ara doesn't stop. It earns her two spankings. *Smack! Smack!*

She cries out and my recording plays on.

"Start again. Slowly, slowly. Mmmm. You are so beautiful like this. All worked up and wet." I count down in my head. *Ten, nine, eight, seven…* all the way to one and then I hear myself say, *"Stop."*

Ara stops this time, like a good girl.

"Slip your fingers in your pussy. Show me how wet you are for my cock."

Ara follows my instructions, her ass wiggling against my groin as she stuffs two of her fingers into her pussy and then lifts her hand up like she's showing me all that glistening desire covering her digits.

I lean forward and suck them clean as my voice filters through the speakers and says, *"Look at you. So perfect and swollen. Ah, ah, ah, I didn't say you could touch yourself again."*

Ara starts laughing because she'd already reached back down to touch herself. She looks over her shoulder at me and my heart stops. She's a messy masterpiece.

And she's all mine.

To my surprise, Ara reaches over and hits the stop button. "You knew what I'd do?"

"I knew what I *wanted* you to do." Which means I love that she's defiant sometimes and obedient others. I spin her around and prop her up on my desk. "There's a lot more if you ever want to hear them. That one was rough because I haven't edited it yet."

Her smile is huge. I'm glad she's flattered and loves what she's heard. "You even edit them?"

"Of course." I nip her neck. "Even if they're only for me, I wanted them as perfect as I could get because they're about you and you're as perfect as it fucking gets."

She's got her hands in my hair again. I love how she pulls the roots and kneads my scalp and drags my mouth wherever she wants.

I drop to my knees and latch onto her pussy, flicking my tongue every which way until I find a rhythm she likes. Then I don't stop until she explodes. No squirting this time, but that's okay. I love that I never know when it'll happen. And I really fucking love that her body craves different actions. It's like she doesn't have just one tried-and-true move that gets her to finish. She needs constant stimulation and a lot of different finger and tongue tricks.

I'm so down for discovering how many combos we can come up with.

"You want a toy?" I ask, rising to kiss her mouth again.

"You have some?"

"Yeah." I have a box. "I've only ever used them as props when recording audiobooks."

Ara's eyes widen when she sees inside my bin. "Oh my God." She plucks out a purple gemstone butt plug. "This is for a recording prop?"

It's clear she doesn't believe me, so I pull the thing out of the box and stick it in my mouth and pull it out with a loud "pop" noise. Then I click on a file further down and hit play on an unedited audiobook I'm still working on. The same noise plays on the speaker that I just made with my mouth.

Ara's head tips back and she laughs so hard, I swear she's crying. "Is this standard practice?"

"Probably not. I'm still learning." I drop the butt plug back in its box. "It's a process I'm still experimenting a lot with. It's likely overkill, but I like being thorough and accurate when possible."

Her eyes glint with wickedness. "That's the second time you've shoved a toy in your mouth."

"That a problem?"

"Nope." She regards me with great satisfaction. "I like it. A lot."

I jostle the box of toys. "Pick your pleasure, Kitty."

"You sure?"

I lift my brow. That question *definitely* earns her a spank. I wouldn't offer if I wasn't sure. I don't ever want her to second guess me or my actions.

Ara blows out a half-breath, because she's happy to have earned another slap on her ass, even if she doesn't know when it's coming. Wiggling her fingers over the top of the box, she plucks out a strand of beads. "I've always wanted to try these."

Be. Still. My. Heart.

I bite back my groan as I dig out the lube and pop the cap.

"Should we…" Ara points at the door which leads to my bedroom.

"We're not using the bed." I slick the anal beads up. "I want your orgasms and your screams, Ara." I gesture at the soundproofing in my closet. "You can let loose in here and no one's gonna hear you but me."

Her lips make this adorable little O-shape.

"Keep your mouth open like that, and I'll have to stuff it with my cock."

She opens her mouth wider.

This woman is perfect. I drop down in the chair and pat my lap. "You ready to play, Kitty?"

Ara straddles me, which requires her legs to hook over the armrests. I'm not sure how that feels on her hamstrings, but she's not complaining. And I'm about to make her feel really fucking good in a second, so…

I reach around and spread her ass cheeks, then circle her tight hole with my lubed-up finger.

Her tits are in my face, and I feel her tense in my lap.

"Relax," I practically purr. "And enjoy."

I want Ara's head to be empty of everything except what I'm doing to her. "Kiss me, Kitty."

She leans in, obediently. When our mouths meet, I gently press the first bead inside her ass. She sucks in air through her nose, sharp and fast. I swipe my tongue across hers, kneading her ass cheeks before shoving another bead inside her. Ara's body accepts them with very little resistance. So long as she stays this relaxed and trusting, it'll be fine.

"You're doing so good," I say in a low tone and press the third bead in. "Such a good girl, letting me fill this ass."

Her breath picks up, and she starts squirming. "I need…"

"Tell me." I twirl the pearls left in my palm, making what's inside her spin a little. "Tell me what you need so I can give it to you, Kitty."

"I need something more inside me." Her cheeks flare. "I feel full and empty at the same time. It's confusing."

Good to know. "How about…" I reach around, and with her spread and straddling me this way, I have easy access to her pussy too. It's a tight fit, but I get my finger in and hook my digit to hit her G-spot.

Ara's reaction is to clutch. Her whole body seizes in this delicious, ultimate clamp down on the pearls in her ass and my finger in her cunt. She grips my shoulders and digs her nails into my skin. I kiss her deeply and shove another bead in. Alternating between hitting her G-spot, sucking on her tongue, and stuffing her ass, I manage to get all seven beads inside her. "You did so good."

She's heavy-lidded and a little cross-eyed. "Feels… feels so good."

I'm glad. It's about to feel a fuck load better.

I've kept the box by my chair and reach in to grab a condom. Look, when I first started narrating audiobooks, I had no clue what I was going to need to make sound effects, but I went with the real stuff because I figured the real stuff would sound the most realistic.

That's not true, but whatever. Audiobooks are still new for me.

I'm just glad to have the condoms within reach. As I rip the package open with my teeth, Ara says, "I have a latex allergy."

Fuck.

We both freeze and I'm not certain what to do.

"I don't want you to use a condom," she whispers. "I know this sounds like bullshit, but I'm clean and I haven't been with anyone in a really, *really* long time."

I want to believe her. There's no reason for Ara to lie, but we're still new here and I don't want to risk fucking something up.

"I didn't sleep with any of my past three boyfriends."

That she'd bring them up at a time like this pisses me off and relieves me at the same time. "They didn't fuck you? Not once?"

She shakes her head adamantly. And it's the look of shame in her eyes that makes my chest cave.

Later, I'll find out why. I'm not tainting this moment with questions about the past.

Time to fess up. "I haven't been with anyone in over three years." Talk about sounding like a loser. I stare at her, making sure my face displays exactly how fucking serious I am. "Last I checked, I was clean. But like I said, that was over three years ago and —"

Ara crushes her mouth to mine and slams down on my cock. We both grunt at the same time. "Holy fuck, you're tight." And drenched.

"Shut up and fuck me, Glitch."

Ara bounces on my dick and it's a miracle we don't break my chair. Neither of us is showing mercy here. It's like years of pent-up sexual tension and long nights of fantasizing about each other have us both unhinging.

"You feel so good," she moans in my ear. Then, instead of bouncing up and down, she swings her pelvis forward and back in a swooping motion, making my dick bottom out inside her and staying that deep. It feels insane.

I've got one hand by her ass, holding her beads in place with a loop at the end around my finger, and my other hand is across her back, holding her close.

She bites my neck and I'm so close to losing it. "Fuck, Ara."

"I'm gonna come," she grunts, using my body for her pleasure.

I lean back so I can watch her grind on me. "That's my dirty girl." I rub her clit with my thumb, hard and fast. "Come all over my cock, Kitty."

This woman owns my soul.

"Oh shit, oh shit." She squeezes her eyes close and then…

Stops.

Her body's shaking. Mine is too. "Are you hurt?"

"N-n-no." She slowly starts to move again, each swerve getting faster and harder against me. Her breaths turn ragged. I feel her body tighten. Then she stops again.

"Fuck!" I drop my head back. "You're gonna kill me."

"At least…" She grinds on me again, "We'll die…" She revs up a little more, "Together…" Ara coils tightly, her breaths sawing, and she squeezes her eyes shut. "I can't… I can't hold it. *I can't hold it!*"

My girl was trying to edge herself.

I shove up from underneath and slam into her pussy hard and fast. All she can do is hold on. Two of the beads pull out from how hard I fuck in her in this position and when I feel her body clamp down, I pull all the beads out, one-by-one, while she explodes around my dick. It's too much, too heady, too tight, and too wet. I careen over the edge with her.

"Gonna fill you up," I growl, dropping the beads to the floor so I can use both hands to fuck her. "Gonna make my cum drip out of you for fucking days, Ara."

She comes again, her inner walls clamping down on my cock with a fierce grip.

I pick my girl up and slam her ass on the desk, driving my cock into her as deep as I can get it. Grabbing her head, I force her to look down. "When you fuck yourself in your studio, you think of this."

"Yes," she pants. "Yes, yes, fuck yes."

I'm going to come again. The base of my neck radiates this wild heat as my balls draw up tight. I pull out and jerk off all over her pussy. "Mine," I growl before stuffing it back into her cunt. The second orgasm is never a big one for me, just a prelude to the much longer, harder third one.

"Oh my God, Glitch." Ara watches as I fuck her. Swiping her fingers along my cum, she shoves them into her mouth and groans. "Do you never stop?"

"Did you want me to?" I drive her closer to another climax and reach down to rub her clit again. Angling just right, I know my dick is hitting her sweet spot. "Is that a yes, or a no, Kitty?"

"Don't stop. *Please*, don't stop!" She claws my back and screams when she comes again. Her thighs quiver around my waist. Her eyes won't stay open. I'm not sure if she can keep going…

But I know how to find out.

I pull out and lick at her pussy, catching every last drop of her desire before giving her swollen clit my undivided attention. I jerk myself while I pleasure her. This is, hands down, one of my favorite wet dreams come to life.

"Gonna come again," she says.

If Ara can still talk, she can still fuck.

I double down on my efforts and hold her belly with my arm, bracing her against the table as she screams. Her cum is sweet and tart and addictive. I'm already dying for another hit.

"Again." I'm relentless in my pursuit to make her explode. It happens, but her fluttering walls aren't as strong with this next climax. My wild girl might need a break.

And a reward.

I jerk myself faster. She watches with a sultry, hungry expression and licks her lips.

"Bring me that hot little mouth, Kitty."

She slips off the table and falls to her knees before me. Opening her mouth, Ara gives me a great target and my dick throbs as ropes of cum hit her mouth, tongue, chin, and tits.

I swear I'm floating when Ara wraps her mouth around my head and does these tight, short little sucks that rob me of fucking breath. "You're insatiable."

She looks up at me, her brow pinched, and I realize she thinks it's in insult. I pull out of her mouth and drop to my knees to kiss her. "So am I." I crush my mouth to hers and don't even care about the mess I've made on her. It's mine. She's mine. It's all mine.

CHAPTER 17

Ara

I'm not sure how Glitch can keep going. I'm not even sure how *I'm* able to keep going. We're both spent and yet we can't seem to stop. When Glitch gets behind me on the floor, and I'm on my hands and knees, I hear the lube top pop and I frown. I'm wet enough. No, I'm a soppy, drenched mess. What does he need more lube for?

Slight pressure consumes my puckered hole. "Mmph." I ease back into his finger, letting him know I want it inside me there. He only circles it a couple of times before breaching the tight ring of muscle. It's such a weird, good sensation that's already got my mind buzzing.

"My Kitty likes her ass played with, huh?" Glitch spanks me once. The sting is quickly soothed away with the stroke of his big hand. "Can I fuck you here?" He thrusts his finger in and out, in and out.

I'm gonna die from how good it feels.

"You can do anything you want to me." I know I'll love it. My fingers claw the rug when he tries to shove another finger inside me. Jesus, I'm not sure I can take it.

"You're doing so well, Ara."

Okay, I can take it.

I suspected a lot of things about myself, but Glitch must hold the skeleton key to all my kink boxes—even the ones I didn't know I had. I wonder how many there are in total.

I look over my shoulder at Glitch. He's on his knees behind me. A riot of tattoos covers his skin. He's so damn delicious, and my body is on fire for him. He runs a hand along my ass cheeks like he can't get enough. I love how turned on he is by me.

And, *man,* are his abs spectacular. I swear I could probably chip a tooth on them. This man has some serious big dick energy.

"Like what you see?" He works his fingers into my backside.

"Yes," I grunt. "A lot."

"Me too." He rears back and spanks me again. "I love my handprint on your ass."

"Then put another on it." I dip down until my face is almost on the carpet and shove my ass up higher for him.

"Fuuuck, Kitty." *Smack*!

I barely feel the burn. His strikes have a big impact with only a little sting. It's enough to make me rock back, which sinks his fingers deeper inside me.

He pours more lube on my crack and all over his dick. Tossing the bottle to the floor, he slicks his massive cock and I'm suddenly wondering if this is a good idea.

"Relax for me."

I don't think I can. He's big. Really big. It's not gonna fit, no matter how much he works me open or lubes us up.

Glitch reads the situation and leans forward, kissing my shoulder while he slides the box closer to us. I hear him rummaging through it, but I'm a little too panicked to ask what he's getting. I hear a click.

Buzzzzzzzzzz.

He presses a vibrator against my clit and makes me come while he stuffs two of his fingers back into my ass, working me open again. "That's a good girl." He twists and pumps and twists and pumps. "So fucking good to me."

My body coils. Blooms.

I feel his fingers slip out again. Then there's a blunt pressure against my ass.

"Breathe," he says.

I concentrate until I'm over concentrating. Overthinking.

He's big. He's really big. Too big. I'm gonna tear. I'm gonna die. It's gonna hurt. I'll never be able to sh—

"Ara." He slaps my ass, snapping me out of my thoughts. "Do you trust me?"

I look back at him again. Sweat drips down my temples and between my tits. I probably look like a drenched kitten. "Yes." And I do. Glitch has read me so well, handled me perfectly so far. There's no reason to doubt him now.

"Breathe for me." He runs the vibrator along my clit. It's enough of a distraction until he's pressing against my puckered hole again. I feel pressure. So much pressure. "You're doing so good, Kitty." More pressure. I'm not even sure if he's got the head in yet and I'm too stunned to ask. The vibrator's gathering more of my attention. My clit is so sensitive, I'm not sure how my nerve endings haven't died yet.

"I'm gonna come," I warn.

I feel dizzy. Floaty. More pressure. More build up.

I gush from the vibrator and Glitch pushes inside me some more. I scream and claw at the carpet. It feels good and wrong and scary and exciting and confusing and I'm gonna pass out if he doesn't do more. "Move. Please move."

Glitch presses into me further. "You feel so good, Kitty." He slaps my ass again, and I'm reeling. I snag the vibrator from him and finally look to see what kind it is. Oh good, a pretty purple rabbit. I crank it all the way up and fuck myself with it while begging Glitch to keep going.

He obliges.

My head's spinning.

He adjusts himself until he's squatting above me. I look between my legs and can see his balls slap against me. I pull the vibrator out and turn it around so the big tip sort of reaches his balls while the clit stimulator hits my sweet spot.

Glitch lets out a delicious guttural groan. His pace quickens.

I want him undone. I want him unraveled and spiraling down this rabbit hole with me. "Come in my ass and watch it drip out."

He makes a million unintelligible noises and my body clenches around him as we both come again. Glitch grabs my ass and spreads my cheeks as he pulls out nice and slow. "Damn that's hot."

I lift up to give him the best view possible. He's so turned on. He's shaking behind me and I love it.

Glitch pushes his finger back in my ass and my toes curl from the sensation. He's a dirty mouthed, wicked unicorn demon. And he just stuffed his cum back into my ass.

"Are you okay?" His mouth is hot on my ass cheek when he bites it.

"Mmm hmmm." I just can't move. My body seems to be locked. "My head's… a little fuzzy."

Glitch moves around and the next thing I know, he's got the door to the closet open and is lifting me off the floor. "I'm gonna take good care of you."

I think I'm drunk. "I feel spacy."

"I know. It's okay. You're going to be okay."

I never said I wasn't. But I can't figure out why I feel this way. "I'm in a subspace, aren't I?" Which means there's going to be a drop.

Glitch kicks his bathroom door open and carries me inside. With gentle care, he sets me on the toilet with the lid down. "How about a bath?"

"That sounds nice." My limbs don't want to cooperate. "I feel like a slug."

He gets the water going and eases me in. I don't want him to let go of me though. Clutching his arm, I squeeze it and say, "There's room for two."

Barely, but we can make it work, right?

Glitch steps in behind me and sinks in. I lay back on his chest and close my eyes. I can't stop shaking, but when he wraps his arms around me, cocooning me in his strong embrace, I settle fast. "I love you," I say. I can't bring myself to overthink how crazy that sounds or how soon it is to say it. We've already tossed it out there twice; a third time won't matter.

He kisses the top of my head and turns the water off with his foot once it's deep enough. "I'm keeping you forever."

"Good." I drift off.

CHAPTER 18

Glitch

"Good morning." I run my fingers down the slope of Ara's waist.

"It's morning?"

"Well…" I glance at the clock on my nightstand. "It's two am. Technically, that's morning." We lost a lot of time in that closet, then the bath, then bed. Ara hasn't had anything to eat or drink in a while, which concerns me. "I've got Chinese food."

Ara sits up immediately and winces.

"Are you sore?"

"A little," she admits, and I feel like a piece of shit because I'd been too rough. I swear I don't know what came over me, and like a fucking fiend, my cock is already straining against my sweats, dying to get back into her somehow. "I'm so sorry. I shouldn't have gone that far with you."

"So I should find someone else to make my fantasies come true?" She tucks her hair behind her ear and tests me. "Okay." The brat swings her legs like she's about to get out of my bed and find someone else to fuck her.

"Don't even try it," I warn.

"Are you going to go that far with me again?"

I stare at her. My brain, heart, and dick don't have a unified answer. "I'll go as far as you'll let me."

"Oh good." She settles back on my pillow. "Then I want to go a lot further next time."

Her answer makes me relieved. "I'm not sure how much further we can get. That was—"

"Epic, mind-blowing, soul-yeeting-out-my-body sex? Yes. Yes, it was."

I'm not sure what to say to that. "Did you just say soul-*yeeting*?"

"Out into the great beyond." She wiggles her fingers in the air. "It's still out there, I think."

I'm really marrying this woman. Today. Right now. Should have yesterday.

"I think I saw God, Glitch."

"Oh, yeah?"

"She was impressed."

I laugh so hard, my voice booms in the bedroom.

Ara props her head up. "You have the *best* laugh."

"So do you." That earns me another big smile. Is it weird that I want to make her happy every second of the day? I want her smiling even in her sleep.

My dick twitches in my pants. She sees it. "You're a unicorn demon, aren't you?"

I have no clue what she means. "I'm just insatiable when it comes to you, Ara." I leave the bed and come back a minute later with a monstrous feast. "I might have ordered most of the menu."

"Ohhh, are there dumplings?"

"Yup."

She flashes a big smile. "Egg rolls?"

"And spring rolls, edamame, wonton soup, egg drop soup, orange chicken, lo Mein, Buddha's delight, and beef with broccoli." I frown, because now I'm not sure it's enough. "I have frozen mochi for later. And… shit, I left the duck sauce in the kitchen."

"I love you," she says around a mouthful of egg roll. "And I'm not saying that because you've fucked me into the next stratosphere or are feeding me. I mean it, Glitch. I love you."

Ara said it in the tub earlier, but that was her subspace brain talking and I didn't know how to respond. But she's with it now and all I can say back is, "I love you too." I crawl across the mattress to kiss her. "I've loved you for a long fucking time." Maybe it won't make sense to anyone else, but it makes sense to us and that's all I care about.

I pull back and flash her a big smile. "I'll be back with more food. And drinks."

She lifts the tray. "Or we can take this out there."

"You sure? I'd rather feed you in bed."

"I'd rather not worry about getting duck sauce on your sheets. Or grease."

I don't care about that, but who am I to tell her where to eat? I can feed her at the table, on the floor, in the tub, and anywhere else she gets hungry. "Okay, hang on."

I grab the tray and balance it in one hand, then help her stand with the other. I want to carry her, but Ara would likely reject the idea. She's too independent to be doted on for long. "Can you walk?"

"Yes, big dicked unicorn demon, I'm fine." But when she takes a step and stumbles, I'm there to catch her. "Okay, maybe I'm a little sore."

Damnit. I drop the tray back on the bed and use both hands to scoop her up and carry her out to the dining room area. I'm pissed at myself for fucking her so hard. And I'm doubly pissed at myself because I plan to do it again.

"I'm okay, Glitch. Really. Seriously, I'm just a little sore."

"Which makes me want to rip my dick off and beat myself with it."

"You'd likely give yourself a concussion. Have you seen the size of your cock?"

She's making light of this? I gently place her down. "I'm really sorry I hurt you."

"Sean."

I freeze at the sound of my name.

"Look at me."

I'm looking.

"I'm *fine*." Ara gives me this look that has me feeling some kind of way. "I'm seriously fine. And if you don't stop doting on me, I'm never fucking you again. Me and the treasure between my thighs will walk right out that door, never to be—"

I shut her up by stuffing my thumb in her mouth. She doesn't bite it. She licks and sucks it. "Did you just threaten me, Kitty?" I pop my thumb out from between her lips.

"Maybe." She bats her lashes at me.

"One."

She flips me the bird and leans back in her chair. "Two." She flips me the bird with her other finger. "Ohhh three."

"Marry me after we eat." I'm only half - joking.

"Okay. But first, I want to meet your sister."

I swear she's only half joking, too. I grab my cell out of my pocket and punch in Erin's number. "Hey, you busy later?"

Ara's eyes grow huge. *"It's in the middle of the night!"* she whisper-yells at me.

Doesn't matter. Erin is like me—a night owl. "Awesome. I'm swinging by with Ara for dinner. Yeah, six works."

Ara cups her mouth.

I hang up. "Erin says she's making tacos. Dinner's served at six."

My girl's cheeks burn red. "You're really gonna let me meet your sister?"

Fuck yeah, I am. Why wouldn't I? "You're the best thing that's ever happened to me, Ara. Of course, you're meeting her. And my nephew, Beetle."

"But… this soon?" She looks terrified. "We're moving fast."

"Are we though?" I tip my head and squint at her. "Really, Ara?"

She blows out a big exhale. "I guess not." My Kitty starts finger-combing her hair. "What if she doesn't like me?"

"What's not to like?"

"I need to shower and change."

"Shower's there, and my clothes are in the spare bedroom closet."

"Glitch!"

"What?"

We stare at each other, holding out for the other to bend and see reason. It won't be me. I'm shamelessly unreasonable when it comes to Ara.

"Fine, I'll take you home so you can change. But I'm totally down for you wearing my clothes. In fact, I'd go a little feral to see you in my sweatpants and t-shirt." I stalk off to grab our food and bring it to the table.

We open all the containers and joke around before she starts asking questions. "So, Erin…"

"Here's our life in a nutshell: Our parents died when I was fifteen. Erin was eighteen. She got legal custody of me and raised me on her own. By the time I graduated high school, she'd gotten pregnant by a jackass who didn't stick around, and she raised Beetle on her own too. His name's really Brendan, but when he was a baby, he'd lay on his back and kick his arms and feet out, which made him look like a beetle on his back. The nickname stuck."

"You guys have a thing with nicknames, huh?"

"My sister definitely does. I just go along with it." I bite into a piece of orange chicken. "Anyway, Beetle's father has nothing to do with him, so I fill that role as much as I can." She needs to know that because Beetle is a huge part of my daily life. These past couple of days were an exception because Erin lost her job and was able to get him from school.

"How did your parents die?"

My heart sinks. "Car accident on a date night."

"Oh my God, Glitch."

"It was fast. I don't think they felt anything." I really don't talk about their deaths. Ara's tears well up and I change the subject. "So, what about you? You have any siblings?"

"Not really."

That's an odd answer.

"My parents spit when I was ten. My dad remarried and started a new family. He doesn't have anything to do with me anymore."

I want to kill him. How can a father walk away from a daughter like Ara? Fuckhead.

"I was raised by my mom. She was an artist like me. Taught high school art, actually. She's who encouraged me to follow my passion instead of getting a degree in some career we both knew I'd hate and settle for anyway."

"Degrees can be overrated."

"I suppose." She plucks at her noodles. "She actually pulled some strings to get me into an art show when I was still in high school. I sold my entire collection that night, plus learned how to network. I was able to pull in two more commissions afterwards."

I'm not at all surprised. Ara's talent is mind-blowing. Gutsy. Bright and bold. It's a direct reflection of her.

"I bet your mom's incredibly proud of you."

"She was."

There it is again… *was*. I don't have to ask; my face does it for me.

"She had a heart attack in the middle of teaching fifth period. They couldn't save her."

I reach out and grab her hand. My heart is broken for my girl.

Ara sighs. "She died covered in pottery clay up to her elbows. I'm convinced there was no better way for her to go. She was in her element, surrounded by students she loved, doing what she was most passionate about."

Fuck me.

"Art's important to you and your mom."

"It's as necessary as breathing," she says. "Sometimes even more so."

I dump more orange chicken onto my plate, rolling her words over carefully. "Are you tied to that warehouse?" I want to know if it has significant meaning to her or if it's just an affordable place she found and settled for.

"Ugh, the warehouse." Ara's face squinches up. "I love it there, but the building was actually sold. We were told about it two months ago."

I pause with the container of steamed rice in my grip. "It didn't look like anyone was moving out." In fact, it was business as usual. Complete with the dogs and bagels.

"We're in various stages of denial. The rent is dirt cheap there and we're allowed to make a mess. It's got nice lighting and free parking. It's an artists' playground. Annnnd will probably turn into some kind of brewery or industry themed condo building now. So depressing."

My brain starts working on a plan. I don't know what I can pull off, but I don't want Ara to lose her art space. If the building's sold, I can't buy it, nor would I want to. It's not in a good part of town, and I'm not into purchasing real estate investments. But I'll come up with something she'll love. "Have you looked into any new spaces yet?"

"No. Like I said, we're all in denial. I keep meaning to, but my routine is to get up and go to the studio and paint, which is all I do. Every time I think I should look around for a new space, it feels exhausting because what little research I've done, I haven't found anything good. It's disheartening."

I bet. Now I have an urge to build a fucking space for her somewhere. "How long do you have left before everyone has to get out?"

"Four more months."

That's not too bad. I was expecting her to say one week. Four months is plenty of time to find her something new that's what she wants and has the security I'll want. This makes me relax a little.

"I've been waiting to hear about this new commission I applied for." She perks up in her chair. "It's to paint a mural in each of the Elementary schools in this district."

I sit back, listening.

"It's not really my style, but I'm trying to branch out. Step outside my box a bit so I can try new things." She shoves an egg roll in her mouth and chews while she talks. "I've been in a massive rut for *months* with my own projects. I was kinda hoping this will get me out of my funk."

"Makes sense." I pick at my food. "Have you had any shows lately?"

"No." She drinks some water. "Not since my mom died. After I sold our house, I paid off her funeral expenses and some other bills and had a little left over. Between that, the money I had stashed away from the two commissions I'd procured, I moved away and came here. I've been on my own with little more than my sad savings and a few other smaller commissions, but it's enough to get by on."

"And you haven't seen your dad at all?" I'm prying, but I don't care. I want to know everything. Pick her apart and see what makes her tick. What motivates her. What crushes her so I can make sure to avoid it or help her work through it in time.

"Nope. He didn't even come to her funeral. Such an asshole." She doesn't seem too upset about it. Maybe she's made peace with her dickhead father's choices. "He was infatuated with my mom, not in love with her." She grabs the rice and dumps some on her plate. "Some guys like the idea of being with a creative person. I have no idea what that fetish would be called, but it's a thing, I think. Like artists and rockstars and creators are some unruly wild animal they can tame and master." She laughs and dumps more orange chicken on her plate next. "That's what my mom would say to me. That we're so full of passion and wildness, we draw them with our magic, and spit them out with our paint."

Sounds possible.

"I have no intention of ever taming you, Ara." I point my chopsticks at her and tilt my head. "But I don't want you to ever spit me out. I prefer watching you swallow."

A smile tears across her face. Then she leans back and crosses her arms, staring at me like she's not sure if she should agree or be a brat about it.

I don't give her a chance to do either. "You don't sleep much, do you?"

"Not really. My head's always going."

"The muse?"

"No." Ara dives back into her food. "The muse has been a silent pain in the ass until yesterday."

Interesting. She drew me yesterday.

"I just can't ever get my head to settle and latch onto anything for long. It doesn't happen when I've got a good handle on my art, but when everything I create doesn't feel right, my brain goes into overdrive and I'm a hot mess about it." She shrugs. "Then I get handsy with myself."

I can tell.

"Can I ask you another personal question, Ara?"

"It's no fun if it isn't personal." She takes another sip of water.

"You haven't slept with your past three boyfriends, including Jason." Not really a question.

"Nope." She slams her water down on the table and wipes her mouth.

"Why?"

"It didn't feel right."

My cock twitches. I must feel right to her if she's this lusty with me. And I'm just beastly enough to swell with pride about it.

"Jason was the worst," she says. "He hated that I wouldn't fuck him."

That has my attention. "Can I ask why not?" It's none of my business, but I hope she'll share anyway.

Ara shrugs. "It didn't feel right. I can't explain it."

"But you stayed with him?"

She pokes at her meal. "I kept breaking up with him, then he'd wear me down and I'd take him back out of pity. It's not a good reason, but I don't have another explanation." Ara sighs and I feel awful for having asked. "I think he thought my not wanting to have sex with him was a game or a challenge or something at first. Then it just became a serious bone of contention between us. Especially because I got myself off a lot. He thought it was dirty. Not dirty, hot. Dirty, disgusting. He once threw all my toys into the dumpster. I had to order new ones online, and those bitches can be expensive."

Especially when you don't have a lot of money to spend.

I want to beat that asshole into the dirt. "Some men have trouble with teamwork," I say carefully.

"God forbid their masculinity is threatened by a fucking battery."

I take another sip of my water. "There's nothing wrong with making yourself come however you need, whenever you need. Fuck anyone who's ever told you otherwise, Ara."

"I once heard if you come three times a week, you can extend your life span." She waggles her eyebrows at me. "I'm gonna be immortal."

"You and me both, Kitty." I raise my glass and we clink them. "Eat up." I tap the side of her plate with my chopsticks. "And drink more water."

We polish off all the takeout, talk and laugh for another hour and then fall asleep in my bed until late morning.

CHAPTER 19

Ara

Two days. It's only really been like two days with Glitch, but I swear it feels like a year. We've fucked, talked, and shared so many deep thoughts with each other it feels like a truth or dare speed date.

I'm sad his parents died when he was so young. I miss my mom every day, but it doesn't hurt like it used to. Death is weird. We all process it differently. I keep hoping I'll get this big job I put a bid in for with the Elementary schools so I can create something I know my mom would love. I was twenty-one when she passed, and I'm grateful for the time we had. We were close.

She'd go crazy for a guy like Glitch. I can just imagine the conversations between them now—especially if she'd seen his shop with all the graffiti art and anime, knowing a senior did it for his portfolio to get into college.

"You're being really quiet, Kitty. What's going on in your head?" Glitch is shaving while I watch. I haven't showered yet. I should, but I don't want to. I'm not ready to wash him off me.

"I'm thinking that my mom would have adored you."

He pauses with the razor to his jaw and stares at me through the mirror. To busy myself, I grab the razor from him. Then I prop my ass up on his vanity and wonder if he'll yell at me for it.

He doesn't.

Jason would have told me the sink would crack from my weight. *Asshole.*

"Can I?" I wiggle the razor.

"Go for it."

I've never shaved a man's face before. It's scary and exciting. "Full disclosure, I've never done this before."

Glitch grins. "We're just popping all kinds of cherries this weekend, aren't we?"

I bite my lip and drag the razor along his face, following the same direction he'd gone with on the other side. We don't talk and the silence is… peaceful. My head's turned off again. The amount of peace Glitch brings me is surreal. I've never felt so calm around anyone before.

When I'm finished, I pat his cheeks with a warm, wet cloth. "How did I do?"

"Perfect," he says, but he hasn't looked at his reflection at all. He's also bleeding in four spots because I did a terrible job. But Glitch hasn't taken his eyes off me since I sat in front of him on this sink.

"You didn't even look."

"Don't need to." He leans in and kisses me.

I'm so in love with this man, it's terrifying. I didn't want to fall this far this fast. But it's too late. I'm already a goner.

"I have to go into work for a while," he says. "Do you want to come with?"

I place the razor on the counter and tuck my hair behind my ears. I haven't brushed it at all. It's a knotted hot pink mess, and I can't seem to care. Not when Glitch keeps looking at me like I'm the prettiest work of art he's ever seen. "Can you maybe drop me off at my studio instead? You can take my car to work, then maybe pick me back up and we can go to my house after that. I'll shower and change and then we can go to Erin's for tacos? Your car's still at my place, so you can grab it then and we can go together or drive separately, or whatever."

I hope he followed that. My brain just skipped around a bit because Glitch looks and smells delicious and I really, *really* want to come again. But I also really, really, *really* want to get back to my studio because inspiration has sparked, and I want to fan these flames.

"Sounds good to me."

"Really?" My request is completely out of the way and a lot of zigzagging around town.

He runs his hand over my tangled hair. "Why is it whenever I say the right thing, you look at me like I'm crazy? What the fuck did the assholes in your life do that make you think you can't have what you want?"

Nailed it.

"That's a lot of driving. I mean, my studio is on the other side of town. It's so much back and forth."

"So? It also means we get to spend more time together. I fail to see a problem here."

I'm going to love this man until the day I die. Fuck that. I'm going to love him even when I'm a shriveled-up corpse in the dirt. Unless I really am immortal, in which case…

"Thanks for always leaving the door open," I say, surprising both of us. "I mean it, Glitch. With Discord… you always kept that chat available." *And private.* "It felt like you were leaving a way open for me."

"I was." His voice is soft. "Which was the coward's way. I should have just asked you to dinner or something."

"No." It wouldn't have worked like that. "I think it was meant to work out like this."

He lifts my chin with his finger. "I could have saved you from dating that twatwaffle Jason, though."

"I needed a pure asshole to compare you to." That came out wrong. "I mean I—"

"I get it," he says, almost laughing.

"Had to reach a low point before skyrocketing to the next planet, you know?"

"If you call me Uranus, I'm spanking you."

"Uranus."

He growls at me, and I swear my lady bits swoon. This guy turns me into a ball of fire with one sound, one touch, one look. I'm so fucked.

And that makes me so damn happy.

He helps me hop down from the counter and spins me around. I can't wait to feel his hand crack my ass cheek. But it doesn't happen. Instead, Glitch kicks my legs apart and shoves his fingers into my pussy. "How are you so fucking wet every time?"

"Have you…" *God, that feels good.* "Have you seen yourself, Glitch?"

"You're all I see," he rumbles against the shell of my ear. "You know, I've imagined you in so many ways, and not a single one of them compares to the real thing, Ara." He shoves another digit inside me, and I go up on my tiptoes.

"What…" *Oh God. Oh God.* "What was your favorite version of me?" *And how do I compare in real life?*

"They were all my favorite. And none of them compare to the real thing. You're the most gorgeous creature to grace this earth. Do you even realize that?"

Hardly. But it's nice to hear. When Glitch works his magic on me, I almost believe it.

"Take a shower with me." He glares at me through the mirror. I gotta admit, we look like a dynamite couple. His dark hair and inked, muscular body make one mighty backdrop for my soft curves and bright pink hair. I don't have any tattoos. Shocking, right? I'd like to get them one day, but want to work on the piece myself, which I haven't been inspired to do at all. Plus, that shit costs money and all my dollars go to paint and rent.

"I don't want to shower."

"Why not?" He doesn't back off. Instead, he runs his knuckles along my rib cage, making my belly flutter.

"I don't want to wash you off me yet."

"Fuuuck, Ara." He drops his head back and his chest expands as he breathes. "Take a shower with me and I'll make you a mess again afterwards."

"Promise?"

"Swear it."

I give in and let him wash me and he even shaves my legs. It's sensual *and* methodical. Just like Glitch.

When I step out of the shower, he's ready with a towel and starts drying me off, even though I tell him I'm perfectly capable of doing it myself.

"Just shut up and let me take care of you, Kitty."

I groan when he dries me off and rubs my hair until it's all tangled. "You're giving me knots!"

"You'll survive." He slaps my ass and makes me squeak. "I like you all tussled and wild looking."

"Ugh." I start finger-combing it. Okay, it's not too awful. And he has really great shampoo and conditioner, which helps.

As I fix myself up, Glitch watches in the mirror. Then he bumps my ass with his thigh, nudging me closer to the counter. "Spread your legs for me, Kitty."

I obey. My heart kicks up, and I hold my breath. Glitch squats down, and I look back at him. He cracks my ass with a hard slap. "Face forward and look at yourself."

Glitch spread my ass cheeks apart and my immediate reaction is to tense. I don't even know what it might look like back there.

"Relax," he growls, his hot breath heating my flesh. "And enjoy."

That man spreads my ass cheeks obscenely and licks me. There. Like right… right there. Sooo right there and holy fucking shit balls on a stick. I bend forward, grunting like an animal about it. It feels insanely good. And when he reaches between my legs and rubs my clit while his tongue circles my tight hole, it feels even better.

My hands press against the mirror.

I come until my eyes cross.

When he rises, I'm still trying to catch my breath. I gawk at my steamed over reflection. He bumps into my backside and reaches over me to swipe his big hand across the condensation and stares at my reflection. "Mine," he growls. Then he spits into his palm and starts to jerk off behind me.

I can't move. I can't breathe. I can't do anything but watch my man get off and when he spurts his cum all over my backside, I swear to fuck I nearly purr about it. I wanted to be messy from him all day and he's delivered.

With a satisfied smirk, he slaps my ass again. I turn and catch his wrist. There's a bit of his cum on his palm and there's no way I'm letting it go to waste. I bring his hand to my mouth and lick it off.

"Fuuuuck, Ara."

"It's Kitty to you."

He smashes his mouth to mine and carries me back into the bedroom.

At this rate, we're never getting back to work.

I think I'm okay with that.

CHAPTER 20

Glitch

I manage to peel myself away from Ara long enough to get her dressed, to her studio, and myself to work. It sucks but knowing I'm picking her up later and going to Erin's for tacos makes it bearable.

I'm addicted to the woman.

I can't wait to see her again. Get my hands on her. My mouth. My dick. It's been six hours and I'm dying over here.

"Heyyyy, Kitty."

She giggles on the other end of the phone. I'm in the back of my shop, door closed, and though I want to jerk off on the phone with her, I won't because I'm not here alone and can't risk it.

"What are you doing?" I ask.

"Painting. What are you doing?"

I can hear her smile through every word she says, and that makes my face split in half with my own grin. "Thinking about fucking you," I confess. "I can't stop thinking about it, actually. I'm hiding in the back of my shop because my dick won't soften."

"I don't think your dick knows how to be soft." She laughs. "I've certainly never seen it flaccid."

And she never will. My blood pumps too hot and strong for her.

"Have you touched yourself yet?" I wait with bated breath for her answer. Will she think I'll be mad if she says yes? I won't. Fuck that, I never will be.

"No," she says after a few beats, but her tone is a little deflated.

"Do it."

"I'm covered in paint."

"Even better. Do it. Right now, on the phone with me."

She makes a beautiful little groan that I want to eat up. "Okay. Let me make sure the door's locked."

"Good girl."

She makes another little moan.

"You're noisy today." And I love it.

"You get me too worked up, Sean. It's your fault."

There she goes, saying my name again, and I have to readjust myself. *Again*. I look over at the door to make sure it's still shut. There's no lock on it, which is what has me on edge. "You need to keep your door locked, always, Ara. Even when you're not working yourself up."

"Okay," she says without missing a beat.

I don't want to be a controlling asshole here, but I'm not about to let Ara be so lost in her painting that she can't hear a fucking intruder, either. All because it hasn't happened yet doesn't mean it won't happen. The risk makes my body tense with the need to be there as her guard dog.

"I usually keep it locked," she says. "I just didn't today in case."

"In case what?"

She's quiet for a few seconds. "In case you popped in."

Fuck. Me. "Take your clothes off."

"Glitch?"

"Hmm?"

"Can... can you maybe call me a slut?"

I slam my hand on the workbench to keep from falling over. "Yeah, I can do that."

She's too much of a praise kitten to be degraded, but I'm willing to toe the line and see which way she likes it best. "Be my good little slut and pinch your nipples."

I hear her suck in a tiny breath.

"I want my teeth on you. Mark you up. Bite and suck your tits."

She makes more noises that drive me wild.

"That's it, my pretty little slut. You want to keep touching yourself?"

"Mmm hmm."

"Go ahead, Ara. Put the phone between your thighs and let me hear how wet you are."

A few seconds later, delicious noises fill my ear. Holy shit, she's soaked. And I'm hard as steel and miles away.

"Ara." Can she even hear me?

"Y-yes?"

I must be on speaker. "What are you thinking about, dirty girl?"

"You," she groans. "Fucking my face."

"Mmmm… you like it when I pump my cock in that pretty mouth? My dirty little slut likes my cum."

"God, yes."

She comes so fast I don't even get a chance to say all the things I had planned. That's okay. There will definitely be other opportunities.

I hear a bunch of shuffling and then her giggle is louder in my ear, which means she's taken me off speaker phone. "Well, that might be a record for me."

I'm already out the door and heading to my car. I want her. Now.

"Glitch?"

"See you in twenty." I jerk my car door open and drop in. "Be ready, Kitty."

• • •

I'm to her in twelve minutes because I break every traffic law. Pulling up to her studio, I take the steps two at a time and notice there's a lot of noise going on. Different music, voices, the dogs.

Don't artists need peace to work? Isn't all this ruckus distracting?

What do I know? I'm just a computer geek who thrives in chaos.

I climb my way to Ara's door and jiggle the handle. It's locked. "Ara?" I knock.

No answer.

I bang louder. "Ara?"

I press my ear to the door, my heart pounding. Why isn't she answering? "ARA!" I slam my fists on the door, ready to rip it off its hinges.

She moans. It's faint, but I fucking hear it. I call her phone. She picks up on the first ring. "Are you already here?"

"Let me in."

She swings the door open but stays hidden behind it. When I see her, I know why. She's still naked. And absolutely covered in paint. Like she'd dipped her fingers in it and touched herself all over the place. Her cheeks are flushed. Her hair's in a messy bun that's sagging to one side. And she has earbuds in.

"I thought I had a little more time." Her thighs are clenched as she scissors them together, seeking friction.

It undoes all my control. "You came again?"

"Yes."

"How many times?"

She pulls her earbuds out. "Including your phone call, four."

Four? That's not enough for me. I'm on her in an instant, lifting her up and damn if she doesn't wrap those luscious thighs around me. I end up pressing her against the window and quickly look out to see if anyone can see us. The alley is abandoned and the building across from us has no windows on this side.

Good. Ara's for my eyes only.

"My dirty fucking slut needs to come more."

She squeaks as I drop down to my knees. Shoving my shoulders between her thighs, I prop her up and start to feast. Her back squeaks against the windows when she writhes. Ara's hot under my touch, her skin damp, and there's a lot of paint on her. I make her come three more times before I pull back.

Her eyes are glassy, lids at half-mast.

"So damn beautiful." I go back for more. She can't get away from me in this position. I have her pinned to the window. My knees dig into the floor as I suck her clit. My zipper is cutting into my rock-hard dick.

"Fuck me," she says. "Fuck me over there."

I look behind me and see she's dumped paint all over the floor.

Setting her down, I strip out of my clothes and pick her up again. I hate not having in her my arms. "Messy, dirty, beautiful girl."

"I'm such a slut for you," she says in a little voice.

"Yeah, you are." I lay her down in the paint. It's not so much that it's a puddle, but there's plenty for me to drag my fingers through and gather enough to smear on her thighs. I write on her: M-I-N-E.

She writes the same across my chest.

Our kisses are frantic when I drive my ready, eager cock inside her. Hooking her legs around my elbows, I lift her up for deeper penetration. She claws the floorboards and cries out.

"No screaming," I growl. "Your noises are only for me."

I dive into her as deep as I can. She lets out another scream.

And has the nerve to laugh about it.

"One." *I love her. I love her. I love her.* If she's going to be noisy just for spanks, then I'll make it so she can't draw air. I fuck her harder, mercilessly.

My plan is a big fat failure when she screams my name so loud her voice cracks. Her inner walls clamp down on my dick and I can't stop staring at all her cream covering the base of my cock. That, along with the paint… it's like Ara's put her stamp on me.

I fucking love it.

I'm getting it inked on me permanently as soon as possible.

My hips are pistons as I chase my release, giving her another climax while I'm at it. My balls tighten, heat spills down my spine, and I roar. I unload so much inside her that it feels endless. My teeth clack when I tense up, another wave of pleasure crashing into me almost immediately. I can't stop fucking her. I don't want to.

"Can't get enough of you." I yank her up so she's straddling me.

My girl's expression nearly blows me over. She's wild and excited and I wish I could capture it with a camera to keep it forever. Her nails dig into my shoulders. I bite her shoulder. Her pussy clenches around my dick and I see stars.

We're like two explosions detonating at the same time.

My heart's pounding and there's a ringing in my ears.

"You're a mess," she says, once she finally climbs off me. I watch her stumble over to a stack of bar towels by her jars of paint brushes. She comes back over with one of the cloths.

I stop her before she can wipe the paint off. "Wait."

I get up and dig my phone out of my pants pocket and snap a picture of my inner thigh.

Then I take a bunch of her. "It's just your face," I say fast. Not that I wouldn't mind nudes of her, but I wouldn't take any of those without permission first. "See?" I show her.

"I trust you."

"Can I have one of you naked?"

She thinks about it for all of two seconds. "Yes."

I don't snap the photo. Instead, I toss my cell back over to my pile of clothes.

"I thought you were going to take a pic of me?"

"I will. One day."

She laughs. "You know I have that painting of me nude, right? I don't mind showing off my body for art."

"Yeah, well, this is for my spank bank. Not sure that's considered art."

Ara's laugh slays me. I swear it's the best sound in the whole wide world.

"So." I rub the back of my neck. "What have you been working on?"

"I can't tell you."

"Ohhh a secret project?"

She saunters over with this wicked little glint in her eyes. "Yyyyup." She pops the p in her answer. "Wanna spank me for not telling you?"

Nope. I want to kiss her again. Which is exactly what I do.

"You really never do get soft, do you?"

I shake my head slowly. "Not since you came into my life."

"This might make grocery shopping awkward."

I glance around and see she's got a half-empty bowl of Skittles on a stool. I stroll over and pluck a red one out and pop it in my mouth. "Is this all you've had to eat today?"

"Mmmm. Yeah. I'm not too hungry." Her stomach growls, saying otherwise. "Okay, so myself just called myself out." She tosses her hands up. "Damnit."

"You got lost in your artwork?"

"Immediately."

That's a good thing, right? Yes, for her mind. No, for her body. Maybe I should grab her something from the burger joint down the road. "If you're on a roll, I can leave. I don't want to derail you."

"You can't derail me, Glitch. Not this time." She taps her temple. "This project is solid. I won't lose it."

"Should I..." I point to the door.

"Only if you're taking me with you." Ara grabs her clothes from the floor. "If I stay, I won't leave, and I really should take a break. I want to paint this one carefully."

"Stepping back is good. Gives you time to process."

"Exactly."

"I'm dying to know what it is."

"RIP you, then." She wiggles back into her clothes, and I'm forced to do the same. "I'm sorry," she says, pointing at my now paint-stained t-shirt and jeans. "Your clothes are ruined."

I pull my shirt back from my skin and frown down at it. It's covered in paint only because I got dressed while I was still wet. And I hadn't wiped much off with that towel she'd given me. "It's an improvement."

It's a wreck. I love it.

Ara dumps her brushes into a jar and adjusts her messy bun. "What did you take a pic of your leg for?"

My grin goes a mile wide. "A secret project."

She flips me the bird and saunters to the door. I follow her. Flick off the lights. Let her lock up.

"You ready to meet my family now?"

Ara frowns. "I wanted to shower and change first."

"Nope. We're going together, just like this."

CHAPTER 21

Ara

We pull up to the most adorable little house with blue siding, a papasan chair on the tiny front porch, a half-dead plant that's only got a few blooms left, and a wind chime made with feathers, sticks and I think bamboo shoots.

I'm nervous. Meeting family is a big deal. I haven't gone this far with any boyfriend since high school and that doesn't count. Everyone knew me back then and I'm far from home now.

Glitch grabs my hand and laces our fingers together. I swear whenever I feel uneasy, he picks up on it and does something subtle to reassure me. Like now, when he gives my hand a squeeze. I can't believe how natural we are with each other. Annnnd I can't believe I'm about to walk into his sister's house covered in paint, with no underwear on.

Glitch insisted on keeping them at his house, so I've been commando all damn day. It was nice, until now.

"Relax." He jiggles my arm. "She won't bite. I promise."

"What if she doesn't think I'm good enough for you?" The words tumble out as we stand on Erin's porch. Glitch turns me to face him. "Never think that about yourself, Ara."

But I do. I always have. I've never felt good enough, not until the day I got my first commission on my own and that's been a while. My insecurities keep trying to land on my shoulder and whisper bullshit in my ear. However, when Glitch glowers—and I do mean *glowers* at me—my system resets because I know better. I do, damnit. I've made it on my own. I've gotten this far. I'm pretty awesome, actually. I've got a concept I'm working on at the studio, and I have the hottest boyfriend in the universe.

"There it is." He winks at me. "There's my Kitty."

I blow out a breath that's only half a laugh.

"Ready?"

"Mmm hmm."

The door opens before Glitch touches the doorknob.

"Uncle Glitch!" A boy grabs his hand and drags him inside first. "Mom said I could get my games back right when you got here, so get in here!"

Glitch gets pulled along by the kid and I'm pulled in by Glitch.

"Erin, come get your unruly demon spawn!"

"Beetle! Lay off! Give your uncle a minute to get through the damn door!"

I'm dragged into a home that's pure chaos. It's the best thing ever. Toys, Pokémon cards, and Nerf gun bullets are scattered everywhere.

"Did you burn the tortillas?" Glitch says, as we cut into the kitchen.

Erin's fanning the smoke detector and the place smells like burnt corn. "Only one."

Glitch lets go of my hand and opens a window and then marches over to the back sliding glass door to open that too.

I stay out of the way, unsure of what I should do. Looking around, I bite my bottom lip. The furniture here is old and well worn. The rooms are cozy and cramped. I absolutely love this house.

"I'm Erin," says a beautiful woman with Glitch's same eye color and big smile. It's easy to see they're related. "That's Beetle."

Beetle waves from the TV, a controller in his hand.

"I'm shocked you're giving him playing rights tonight." Glitch strolls back to the kitchen where he left me.

"I figured this was a good way to keep him occupied so we can actually talk about things other than Pokémon for a change." Erin looks at me and shrugs. "He's only allowed a half-hour of screen time a day *if* he has good grades, so this is a super big deal to him."

What kid wouldn't be psyched for unlimited game plays for a night? I can hardly blame him.

"But it's for *AFTER HE EATS ALL HIS DINNER!*" she yells.

"I willllllllll!" Beetle yells back.

My God, they're loud. As someone who spends most of her days and nights alone, it's a shock to my system. It's nice.

"Okay!" Erin claps her hands. "Glitch, make the guac. Ara?"

"Yes?"

"Get busy on the margaritas."

Glitch plucks three avocados from a bowl and starts juggling them. Two fall on the floor almost immediately.

Erin rubs her temples. "Oh my God, this dinner is going to be awful. Stop bruising the food, asshole."

"I'm just trying to keep the bar as low as you do, Erin. Can't eat perfectly good guac with burnt ass tortillas."

She throws a jalapeno at him. He tosses it back at her.

"Welcome to family dinner, Ara." Erin flashes me a big smile. I can't lie, she's making it easy to like her. A lot.

Dinner goes off without another fire or even a cut finger. My margaritas are strong, but Erin swears they should be stronger since she has to put up with Glitch for the night. It's obvious she's teasing because they act more like best friends, not brother and sister.

Glitch and Beetle strike up a conversation about math, and Erin rolls her eyes and turns her focus solely on me. "My brother is a terrible influence."

"Clearly." I nod, watching how great he is with his nephew. They're going over fractions. After a few minutes, they stop talking and turn to Erin.

"Mom. Can I now?"

Erin narrows her gaze at Beetle, then his plate, then to Glitch. "Two more bites and then yes, you may."

Beetle stuffs his mouth with just the ends of his soft taco shell and leaves the rice, beans, and guac on his plate. "Thank youuuuu!" He shoots off from his chair. "You coming, Uncle Glitch?"

He's torn. We can both see it. "Just for a minute," he says after I wink at him. "But I'm here on a *date*, Beetle. You're cramping my style."

"You have no style."

"Ouch." Glitch frowns and clutches his heart as he stares at his nephew. "You cut to the quick, man. That hurt."

Beetle cracks up and runs into the living room. Glitch chases him and manages to catch Beetle in a few seconds. Then he flips the boy upside down and pretends to shake his brains out of his ears. Beetle's peeling laughter fills the house.

Erin and I burst out laughing. She holds her chest and leans forward, nearly dipping her hair in the sour cream. "Wow. How strong are these things?" She takes another sip of her margarita.

"You just complained they weren't strong enough!" I laugh.

"I mean..." Erin takes another sip. "Mmm yeah, this is fucking yummy."

"Language!" Glitch hollers.

Erin mouths *"Fuck You"* back at him silently. "It's been a while since I've felt this giddy. I don't think it's the tequila. I think it's the company."

I know the feeling. "It's wonderful to meet you. This dinner was amazing." I get up and start collecting the dishes.

Erin places two more plates in the sink and leans against the counter. "So..." she shoots me a narrowed gaze. "When are you two getting married?"

I almost drop my glass. "Ummm."

"Look, Glitch has never brought a girl home before. Not ever. If you aren't the one, you wouldn't be in my kitchen right now."

I glance into the living room. Glitch's back is to me. Can he hear us talking?

Erin goes on. "And he's covered in paint. That's not like him either."

My stomach twists.

"He's controlled and methodical, always. *And* a neat freak."

Glitch's voice rises from the living room. "I can hear you, Er."

"Good!" Erin rolls her eyes at me playfully. "He's an asshole about the way I load the dishwasher."

"There's a method!" he barks back. Glitch doesn't even bother to turn around. All we see is the back of his head on the couch, and Beetle's equally dark head of hair next to him.

Erin shouts back, "There's gonna be a method to how I kick your ass next time you rearrange my silverware!"

Glitch flips her the bird over his shoulder and Beetle has somehow crept up behind us to snag a lime wedge. He looks up at me and smiles. "They're always like this. You'll get used to it." He shoves the lime wedge in his mouth, between his front teeth and smiles at me again, with big, green lime teeth, before dashing back to the couch again.

Glitch gawks at him. "Whose side are you on, man?"

"My mom's."

"Traitor." Glitch ruffles his hair, and I see they've pulled up Minecraft.

"He's been bullied a lot in school," Erin says in a soft tone. "Some kids apparently stole all his stuff in some world on there. He's been really bummed about it."

"Some kids are total assholes."

"Some adults are total assholes."

"Fair." We clink our glasses and finish clearing the table.

Erin waves her hand over the filled sink. "Leave 'em. I'd rather sit outside and talk."

I follow her to the back patio. The small, fenced-in yard has a bike leaning against a tiny shed, and there's a miniature half-pipe ramp and trampoline. "Your house is fantastic."

"Thanks." Erin plops into a chair. "It was our parent's house."

My heart sinks a little.

"Beetle's in Glitch's old room, which he loves. Fucker had the bigger closet when we were growing up."

"Did he even use it for clothes?"

"Of course not."

We both laugh. Guess something's don't change since his current closet is a recording studio.

Erin tilts her head. "Tell me more about you, Ara."

"There's not a lot to tell. I'd rather hear more about Glitch, honestly."

"Well, I guess I'll start at the beginning." Erin slams her now empty margarita on the table between us. "He didn't have many friends growing up. Got bullied a lot for his voice."

White hot anger burns through me. "*What?*"

"They used to call him Deep Throat. It was a fucking nightmare. And it only got worse once our parents died." She pauses. "You knew they were dead, right?"

"Mmm hmm."

This must surprise her because Erin's eyebrows shoot to her hairline. "He never talks about them."

But he did to me. I cautiously take another sip of my drink before setting it down.

Erin pulls her hair back and ties it with a hairband. "After our parents died, I raised him, and now he's helping me raise my son. We're as close as it gets."

"Close enough to call you at two thirty in the morning about dinner."

"I don't sleep much. Neither does he. We're never on *Do not disturb*." She rubs her eyes and yawns.

"Were you serious when you said he's never brought a woman home before?"

"Dead serious, Ara."

"Not even in high school?"

"He didn't go to prom. He's never dated a girl longer than a minute, and I can't even remember the last time that was. It's been forever. I was starting to lose hope."

My brows knit together.

"He's amazing, and no one sees it because he's always working, or with me and Beetle."

"He loves his job. And you guys are important to him." Erin lets out a long exhale and stares up at the sky. "He shouldn't have to fill the role of the person who walked out on us."

"I'm sure Glitch doesn't do anything without wanting to do it with his whole heart. It's obvious he loves you both a lot."

"He does. But he needs a life." She glances behind her. Through the window, we can both see them playing the video game. "He had a full scholarship to MIT. Got his degree and, in full Glitch-the-control-freak fashion, he turned down every job offer and stayed back to be with us. Opened his computer shop instead of moving onto bigger, better things."

"Maybe he considers what he's built bigger and better. I can't imagine him working an office job. Or answering to someone else."

"You've got that right." Erin shakes her head, sighing. "By the time Beetle was four, Glitch expanded his store and created a sanctuary for kids to go to after school. He even has tutors set up to help some of them who are struggling with certain subjects."

"Wow."

"He didn't tell you any of that?"

I shake my head. "We're still pretty new with each other."

"Not that new. You're the one he plays with online, right? With Trey?"

I nod. I can't believe she knew that. It makes me feel warm inside that Glitch might have mentioned me to Erin, even when we were virtually nothing.

"He probably wouldn't have bragged about his accomplishments to you. He sucks at talking about himself. My brother is all about lifting others up. It's his method of coping, I think. At least, that's what his therapist said back when I would make him go when he was in high school."

I don't doubt it. "He's an amazing guy."

"Yeah, he is. So please don't break his heart." Erin heads inside, coming back out with two glasses of water a moment later. "Anyways..." She hands one over. "Sometimes I think he wishes he'd been the oldest so he could take care of me. I know he stuck around because he felt indebted. I wish he wouldn't, though."

"You wish he hadn't stuck around?"

Erin shakes her head. "Feel indebted."

"You had to grow up fast. I'm sure he wishes it was different for you too."

Erin shrugs. "We made the best of a terrible thing. Can't do any more than that. Getting pregnant with Beetle put a wrinkle in my life plans, but I wouldn't trade him for the world. Instead of college, I got to keep this house, which I love, and I used the money set for my education to put towards raising my son. Glitch's portion of the college fund was used to build his business since he had a full ride to college."

I'm not at all surprised he got a full ride to MIT. "He's a genius."

"Totally." Erin fidgets as she watches them through the window. "I think his college years were his best and worst years, to be honest. He hated being away from me and Beetle. Came home as often as possible to help me. But he met guys there who are still his friends, and I'm forever grateful for Trey. He's great at getting Glitch to step out of his comfort zone."

I'm grateful for Trey too.

"Glitch stuck close to home after graduation and is a huge part of Beetle's life." She eyes me up. "Are you a fan of kids?"

"Love them." And I do. "My mom was an art teacher."

"Sweet!" Erin chugs her glass of water. "I miss getting drunk."

"I wouldn't want a hangover with a kid around."

"He's so loud. Why are boys so loud?"

Glitch pokes his head out from the sliding glass door. "What are you two talking about?"

Erin rolls her eyes. "You, asshole."

He stomps into the backyard and tips my chair back to kiss me upside down. "How drunk are the two of you?"

"Not even a little," I say.
"Can you help us?"
I stand up. "Yeah, sure, with what?"

CHAPTER 22

Glitch

As far as dates go, I have no clue how to rank this one. Ara fits right at home with us. And when she grabs a controller and starts building a castle, I swear my heart explodes.

Ara settles in between Beetle and I on the couch, automatically invested. "How big do you want it?"

"I don't care. Just make it have lava floors."

I raise my brow at Beetle, and he quickly adds, "Please and thank you."

I slip away to talk with Erin while they play. "So?" I lean against the doorway to the kitchen. I wish she'd repaint the place. It needs a serious remodel.

"So?"

"You like her?"

Erin deadpans me. "It doesn't matter what I like, Sean."

Yikes. She used my real name. "Do you?"

"I've never seen you smile so much at dinner before tonight." She hands me a towel and we start the dishes. "I've never seen you covered in paint before, either."

"Ara's..."

"Good for you."

"I think we're good for each other."

"Then you better not let her go." She hands me the first dish to dry.

By the time we're done cleaning up, I head back to the living room and stop dead in my tracks. Ara's laying on her belly, facing Beetle, and they're sketching something on a big piece of paper from my sister's arts and crafts stash.

"What's this?" I squat down for a better look.

"Ara's showing me how to draw anime."

Erin creeps over quietly. "Holy shit."

Yeah. Holy shit is right. Beetle has a night of endless video games and he's chosen to turn it off to draw.

"*Marry her*," Erin whispers before shoving me aside to sit on the floor. "Let me see, Beetle!"

I love this. I love this so much it hurts.

"I'm doing Pikachu. She's doing Squirtle."

Ara smiles at Erin. "Beetle says he wants a collage in his room of all his favorites. I promised to come back and help him. It'll be an after-dinner project."

"You, Ara, are a gift from the gods." Erin ruffled her son's hair and kisses his head. "This looks amazing, buddy."

"I already screwed it up."

"There are no mistakes in art," Ara chides. "It's impossible to screw up."

"Well, what's that then?" Beetle jabs his pencil at a blurry erased spot by Pikachu's ear.

Ara tilts her head and studies it. "Looks like an opportunity to me." She squints and tilts her head in the other direction. "Maybe there's a Poke ball behind him, and that," she taps her pencil on the blur mark, "is the dark part of the ball." She looks at him. "May I show you?"

"Yes, please."

I'm so proud of this kid right now. He usually tosses a fit when things aren't "just so" which is a flaw I fear he gets from me. But he's not freaked about it right now.

Ara's the reason.

"Okay, look." She quickly sketches out a ball and the blurry spot that's gray is now incorporated into it. "See? And when we color it in, this will be black." Next, Ara draws a random line across the top of her Squirtle head. "What can this maybe be?"

Beetle stares at it. "A hat?"

"Awesome idea!" Ara draws a top hat on Squirtle's head, and I sit down on the couch. It's either that, or my legs are going to give out.

"Where's your bathroom?" she asks.

It takes me a second to find my voice. "Upstairs, second door on the right." When she leaves, I look over at Erin.

"This woman is a fucking *unicorn*, Glitch."

"Better put a ring on it," Beetle adds. Then he looks up and shrugs. "What?"

"You should probably get to bed, little dude."

And we should probably get out of here. It's late, and even if my sister doesn't sleep well, she could probably do with a little quiet time. "How's the job search going?"

"It's coming along." She yawns and elbows me. "Don't worry."

I can't help but worry.

"Oh my God!" Ara squeals from upstairs. "Oh my God! Oh my God! *Glitch*!" She races down the steps so fast, I'm afraid she'll fall.

I'm immediately on high alert. "What's wrong?"

"I got it!" Her eyes are huge as she holds her cell out to me. "I got the job! The elementary school murals! Holy crap, I got it!" She's so elated she's shaking. And her joy is contagious.

Erin claps enthusiastically. "What am I excited about?"

I lift Ara from the ground and spin her. "Of course, you got the job! You're insanely talented."

"Someone tell me why I'm clapping!" Erin shouts louder, swept up in our excitement.

I put Ara back on her feet and she's fucking beaming with excitement and pride. "I put a bid in to paint a mural in each of the elementary schools. It's not a huge commission, but…" She looks up at me and I can hardly breathe from how fast my heart's pounding. "My mom's going to be so proud of this. I've... I have so many plans... the colors, and OH! The surrealism and... she *loved* that stuff... but I'm adding my own twist with these *big* flowers and this huge—" She stops and covers her mouth. Her eyes get even bigger. Then she starts to cry, and I wrap her in my arms.

"You've got this," I say against her hair.

She clings to me, still shaking. "I can't even believe I got it."

I don't know why. Her talent is beyond anything I've ever seen. "Come on." I pull Ara back and steer her towards the front door. "Let's get out of here."

"Where are you going?" Erin asks.

"To her studio. She's not going to sleep until she gets some of this excitement down on canvas."

That earns me a massive smile from Ara. She rushes over to hug Erin and Beetle goodbye and promises to be back for dinner sometime soon, and then we're in the car heading to her studio again.

She keeps staring at her phone, reading the email over and over. But she's quiet. That energy has crackled into something spikier. I can't tell what it means.

"What if I fail?" she whispers. "What if my idea doesn't translate like I want it to?"

"You won't and it will."

She's not convinced. Her insecurity demons are rallying. I pull over and throw the car in park. "Look at me, Ara."

She stares into her lap where her phone is.

"Hey." I gently cup her chin, making her face me. "Didn't you just say there are no mistakes in art?"

Her bottom lip quivers.

"You're going to slay this. And then you're going to slay the next project and the one after and the one after. Do you know how?"

She shakes her head.

"By telling those demons barking all that negative bullshit in your head to shut the fuck up. You one hundred percent have this. They loved your proposal, or you wouldn't have been picked."

"Maybe I was the only one who submitted."

"So what if you were? That doesn't say shit about your talent. What you do with your opportunity will. I can't wait to see it."

She stares back at her phone. "Thank you."

"Thank *you*," I shoot back. "I'm so honored to get to be a part of this, Ara. Seriously. Seeing you this happy is… fuck, it's… it's everything."

My girl lunges into my chest and kisses me so hard our teeth clack. When Ara leans back, she's grinning again. "I'm gonna do this."

"Yes, you are."

"It's going to be amazing."

"Damn straight it is."

"And then more commissions will roll in and maybe I'll even get another exhibit somewhere."

"Abso-fucking-lutely."

She shimmies back into her seat and reaches over to unbuckle my belt. "I want your dick in my mouth."

"I will never say no to that."

Her hot tongue is on me a moment later. She sucks me off so hard I see stars. "Holy shit, I hope you get never-ending commissions." Ara laughs with a mouthful of my cock, and it vibrates down to my balls. "Fuck." My hips jack up and my dick crams down her throat. She gags. I growl.

Her cell goes off with a text.

We both ignore it.

She draws me in and does wicked things with her tongue that make me think of glorious ways to return the favor. "Such a good girl." I hold her hair, guiding her head up and down my length. She uses one hand to pump me and licks my head like it's a fucking lollipop.

"Give me your cum, Glitch." She licks and sucks and draws me in until I hit the back of her throat again.

"Just like that," I say. "Keep sucking it just like that and I'll give you what you want." I don't last long. "Swallow it all." I groan just as my cock jerks in her mouth. She doesn't miss a goddamn drop and when she lifts her head, she swipes her finger along the corners of her mouth and licks it clean. I run my thumb across her bottom lip. "Good girl."

Her reaction when I talk like this will never get old. Her pupils are big, her cheeks get all rosy, and she squirms. "Take me back to my studio and fuck me?"

"Yes, ma'am."

She giggles and sits back in her seat. Picking her phone up, Ara stares at the screen again. Only this time, her face pales when she clicks on her newest text.

The energy in the car shifts again and the hairs on the back of my neck stand on end. "What's wrong?"

Ara starts to panic. Her breaths punch out of her in short spurts. "No. No, no, no." She holds the phone to her chest so I can't see it.

"Ara, what is it?"

"I'm…" She unbuckles her seatbelt and fumbles with the doorhandle, only to tumble out of the car.

Jesus. What the fuck? "Ara!" I scramble out of the car. She's running. Running and crying and freaking out and I have no clue why. "Ara, stop!"

She doesn't. I chase her down and pull her back with my hands around her waist. "I'm going to kill him!" she scream-cries. "I knew it! I knew things were going too good. Nothing this good happens to me for real."

I'm so confused I don't know where to start. "Talk to me."

She crosses her arms and cries harder.

"Ara, goddamnit, *talk to me!*"

She shoves her phone in my face, and my heart falls out of my ass. Then my blood turns to toxic, fiery poison.

A video plays on her screen. It's Ara, in her bed, masturbating. Clip after clip after clip.

It doesn't take a genius to know who sent her this.

Fucking Jason.

"He's going to ruin me," she sobs. "I'll lose the school's commission if this leaks."

I'm seeing red.

"I don't even know how he could have gotten this!" She clutches her hair. "How could he have videotaped me?"

I need to stay calm. Think. Breathe. "It's okay." I'm not sure it is. "We'll handle it." I'm not sure she'll like how I plan to handle it. "We'll figure it out."

"You're not…" She sobs again. "You're not mad at me?"

I think I've snapped. I must be mad. Insane. Off the rails. "Why would I be mad at you?"

"I don't know!" she scream-cries at me.

Jesus fucking Christ. Her exes have done such a head job on her. I'm going after every single one of them.

Starting with Jason.

CHAPTER 23

Ara

I was so happy. For a whole three days, I was the happiest I've ever been in my life. And now comes karma's painful balance.

I stare at the message again. *"If you don't come back to me, I'll make sure everyone knows what a disgusting slut you are."*

Jason could post this on porn sites. He could send it to anyone I might try to do business with.

I don't care about my body being on display. I paint myself naked all the time. And porn is porn, but that's not what bothers me. It's that he's violated my privacy. Stole private moments to use against me. It could cost me everything I hold dear.

It could cost me Glitch.

He has no reason to believe me when I say I didn't know Jason recorded all this. And I can't even figure out how he did it. But the angle of each video is almost the exact same, and that's when it clicks. My blood runs cold. "Take me home."

Glitch hasn't said a word. He strangles the steering wheel while he drives, and I'm scared I've already lost him. I'm a mess. No one wants a drama-infested dumpster fire for a girlfriend. It's too much.

I'm too much.

When Glitch leaves me, I won't blame him.

I squeeze my eyes shut. *Breathe, Ara. Hold it together.*

We're at my apartment in less than five minutes. I can't believe I live so close to his sister. I'm not sure what to say or how to act or what to do, so I go with, "I'm sorry."

"Stop. Apologizing." His voice is intense. Dark. Strained. Glitch hasn't looked over at me since we got back in the car.

"I…" *Stop apologizing.* He's right. I didn't do this. I did nothing wrong. And I'm not saying sorry on behalf of a bastard who I hate and who's actions I have no control of. I just need to figure out how to make it not get worse. "Will you come up with me?"

Glitch fumbles with the door handle, his gaze still deadlocked straight ahead. I think he's glitching, and it makes me feel worse. He hates this as much as I do.

His gait eats up the asphalt as we head to my apartment. Glitch swings the lobby door open for me and takes the steps fast, leaving me several paces behind. I only half expect Jason to be waiting at my door, a smug smirk on his stupid face because he thinks he can best me. Maybe Glitch expects him too, with how fast he makes it to my door.

But Jason's not there.

"Open the door, Ara." Glitch's voice is still strained. He still won't look at me.

Why won't he just look at me?

I shove my key in the lock and my hands shake too much to make it work right. He places his hand over mine and whispers, "Relax. Breathe."

I'm not even sure if he's saying it to me or to himself. Probably both. I let out a long exhale and turn the key. The door opens. My home is quiet.

Empty.

Glitch storms into my bedroom and rips the laptop off my desk. Holding it under his arm, he heads back out and I panic. "Where are you going?"

"Get in the car."

"But where are you—"

He stops short. "I'm going to find out how he did this. Then I'm going to ruin him."

He's not even joking.

We head to Glitch's in dead silence. I'm scared he's going to end this with me. I'm scared my reputation will be destroyed somehow. I'm scared for things I'm not even sure I understand. My head won't stop overthinking. I'm angry and tired and fed up.

Glitch gets out of the car and storms over to my side. I barely get the door open when he swings it the rest of the way. I climb out. His grip on my laptop is so strong, I swear he's going to crack the case. Before I can take one step, he kisses me. Hard. Fierce.

It resets my brain. Reassures me that we can handle this nightmare.

If he kisses me, it means he's not going to run, right?

"Come on," he growls, but his tone isn't nearly as deadly anymore. It brings me a little relief. We enter his house, and I follow him into the living room like a lost puppy. He storms through it and takes the steps up to a spare bedroom where three massive monitors are lined across a desk. He boots up all the machines and plugs in my laptop.

There's so much going on, I'm not sure if he's booting up a laptop or a launching goddamn space shuttle.

Glitch opens another sleeker laptop and does something else with that one. Suddenly all this code shows up on the screens.

"Will you take me to his house?" He asks while clicking away. Five screens are now going at once, all with different codes and shit. I can't make sense of any of it.

"I don't know where he lives anymore." That's the truth. "He was supposed to relocate to Alabama for his job, but I'm not sure what happened. He's still around, but... not at his old place anymore. I saw a for sale sign on it a while back saying it was sold."

"Okay."

That's all he says. *Okay*. Like it's no big deal. Not a problem. Totally fine.

His fingers fly across two keyboards at once. Jason's photo shows up on the far-right screen. It's from his work badge. Oh my God, did Glitch just hack into Jason's company's database? All these other thumbnails start to pop up on another, but I don't look at them.

I hug myself and turn away. I can't stomach seeing that asshole's face, even in a photo.

"Jesus." Glitch shoots up from his seat so fast, he knocks his chair over. His fingers fly faster across the keyboards. It sounds frantic and chaotic.

And methodical.

I keep my back turned. My palms are so sweaty. I don't know what he's found, but it's set him off. I can feel the tension roll off Glitch, but I don't make a peep. And I'm too scared to look.

More clicking.

"He put a program on your laptop," Glitch says calmly. "It records even when the screen is off." He clicks more buttons. Types more things. Cusses a lot more.

"He *gave* me that laptop," I explain. "After he kicked my gaming computer and broke it, he gave me the laptop as an 'I'm sorry' present."

Glitch's shoulders tense, but he doesn't stop typing. I can't bring myself to look at the monitors, so I focus on Glitch. His eyes dart from one screen to the next, his face glowing from the different screens flashing.

It's scary and hot seeing him work like this. I suddenly don't care what he's doing, I just don't want him to get caught. Because I'm not going a day without this man, mark my motherfucking words.

He shoves back from the desk and slams my laptop closed. The monitors all turn off. "Let's go."

I follow him. "You found where he lives?"

"Yup."

"And we're going to go there?"

"Yeah." Glitch stops. "Unless you don't want to come with me? But until I get a security system on your doors and windows and in your studio, I really don't want you at either place alone."

This can't be happening. Cool night air hits my face as we step outside. Glitch hadn't parked in his garage. He parked in the driveway this time. I'm almost to the car when my phone rings. I pull it out of my back pocket as dread coils in my gut. *Unknown number.*

Glitch's deep voice shoots confidence down my spine. "Answer it."

I refuse to give Jason my fear. Or my pain. I refuse to give that jackass one more ounce of my energy. I hit the answer button and say, "Go fuck yourself, Jason."

"Ara, listen to me, baby. I won't post the video, I swear. I just sent it to you so you'd answer your phone and talk to me. I miss you so much, I'm dying inside."

"You're sick. You're a sick, twisted—"

"Jason," Glitch says after taking the phone from me. "It's nice to finally talk to the man who ruined his chances with my Ara."

My heart's in my throat. I'm dizzy and frazzled.

"Thank you for the video compilation. My girl's *fire*, isn't she? She's fucking hot when she touches herself."

I hear a door slam on the street. Next thing I know, Jason's storming across the cul-de-sac, cell phone still up to his ear.

Oh my God, he must have put a tracking program on my laptop too!

I'm going to be sick.

Glitch hangs up my phone. The smile he's wearing is nothing short of feral. He's not at all shocked to see Jason here.

"Ara," Jason barks, looking half-crazed. Dressed in a suit, his tie loose around his neck, shirt untucked, he stalks closer. "I need you, baby."

I step back. "Jason, you need to leave me alone."

His face contorts with anger. "*You* need to do as you're told and get the fuck over here."

Glitch steps between us. "Come near her," he warns, "and I'll tear your goddamn face off."

Jason's got this awful, smug, shit-eating grin on his face as he strides over to us, raises his fist, and swings at Glitch.

I'm so stunned, I can't move.

Glitch doesn't block the hit. Doesn't duck. Doesn't even rock back when Jason clocks him in the face. "She's *mine*." Jason barrels into him, roaring like a maniac, driving Glitch backwards. He swings out again, only this time Glitch doesn't give him another freebie. He blocks the punch with one hand, and cold cocks Jason in the jaw with a hard left hook.

Jason drops instantly. His head hits the ground, skull smacking on the cement.

"Holy shit!" I hope he's not dead. Glitch can't go to jail for murder. I don't know what to do! Bending down for a better look, fear spikes my bloodstream when I see blood.

"Don't touch him, Ara." Glitch pulls his phone out and calmly holds it up to his ear. "I'd like to report an assault." He gives the location and steps back a few paces. I can tell he's furious and ready to snap. He hangs up after answering several questions, and then the flashing lights appear minutes later.

Cops arrive and take our statements.

"We were on our way out when Ara's ex came out of nowhere and attacked us."

One cop asks, "Do you want to press charges?"

Glitch looks over at me, giving me all control. I know he'll respect whatever I decide. My stomach clenches. I can't believe this just happened. "Yes."

I absolutely want to press charges. And when I see the red mark on Glitch's face start to swell, I wish I could murder Jason for hurting him. For all the shock, anger, and nausea rolling through me, having Glitch stand strong at my side, remaining calm with the cops and being a rock for me, gives me strength.

Glitch holds the laptop under his arm as he laces his freehand with mine. His squeeze reassures me.

"I have video of the attack if you want it." Glitch points at the surveillance cameras he has set up that I never even noticed.

"Yeah. That'll be a help." One of the police officers hands him a card. "Email me the clip. We'll be in touch."

They take Jason away in an ambulance.

And that fast, my ex is gone, and the cops drive away.

They don't know about the stalking. They don't know about the video clips Jason made of me. They don't know about anything except Jason showing up and attacking Glitch. There's a reason Glitch didn't say anything more to those cops. And I let him take the lead on this because I'm not sure what to do and I have no clue what else Glitch saw when he'd hacked into Jason's stuff to find him. All I know is Glitch is protecting me. From what, I'm not even sure anymore.

Fucking Jason.

I look at the laptop under Glitch's arm. Rage consumes me and I rip it away from him. Holding it over my head, I smash the fucking thing against the curb, over and over and over. I bust it to pieces until it's scattered over the sidewalk. Then I stomp on it. Scream at it.

It doesn't help make this awfulness go away.

"Ara."

I feel sick. "What did you see?"

Glitch doesn't answer at first.

"What else did he do?" I scream.

"He had underage porn on his computers," Glitch says cautiously. "Both at home and his office."

Glitch's reaction upstairs now makes more sense. *All those thumbnails...were they pics of what Glitch is talking about?* I fear so.

Staring at the pieces of computer all over the ground, I spit on it and stumble back. I need a shower. I feel disgusting. "What are we going to do?" We have to report it. But if we report it, we'd have to admit that we hacked into Jason's stuff. I don't want Glitch in trouble.

I also don't want Jason to get away with what he's done.

This is a nightmare and a half.

Glitch stands stiff as a board. "I've locked his computers both at home and office so he can't get into them. I'm going to anonymously report him to the Cyber Tipline and give them the new password to his computers. They'll have to investigate it and see for themselves and take it from there. I can also follow up with the Chief, just to make sure Jason doesn't slip through the cracks and get away with anything."

"You won't get in trouble for hacking?"

"I'll make sure I don't. Since his kid comes to my shop every day after school, we're friendly and he respects me. The Chief's not going to bust me for this if I'm helping him put a monster like Jason behind bars, but I'll be cautious about my report to him just in case. First, let the Cyber Tipline do their job. It might be all that's needed to put Jason away for a good long while."

I shake my head because I no longer trust myself to speak.

While Glitch makes the call and reports it, my heart lurches in my throat. I'm shaking and numb.

I dry heave on the curb.

"Shit." Glitch is on me in an instant. "I've got you." He holds me tight and eventually we make our way back inside his house. I just want this horror erased from my brain. At least Jason is going to jail. I hope he's never acted on his…

I run into the bathroom and dry heave again.

Glitch barely makes a sound as he holds my hair back for me while I retch in the toilet. Once I think I'm able to stand, I splash cold water on my face while he rubs small circles on my back. "What about the video of me?" It feels stupid to ask in the grand scheme of things.

"Taken care of."

"How?"

"Erased."

I whole-heartedly believe him. Glitch wouldn't lie and he wouldn't leave any loose ends. I brush my teeth and splash water on my face again. How did this go from the best day to the worst night ever? "I'm sorry everything went sideways."

What am I even doing?

"Ara."

I squeeze my eyes shut. The way he says my name breaks my heart. I'd do anything to re-write the past hour.

"Ara." He spins me around and I feel like I'm shriveling. "Heyyyy," he says in this deep, wonderful tone. Glitch dips his head down so he can capture my gaze.

My fists clench his shirt and I jerk him forward until our mouths collide.

CHAPTER 24

Glitch

Take it slow.

She kisses me like I'm the air she breathes.

Maintain control.

She kisses me like I'm her motherfucking lifeline.

This is crazy, and I need to not short-circuit.

Ara rakes her fingernails down my arms, up my chest, around my neck and down my back. She's everywhere. Frantic. Desperate.

It took everything in my soul to not beat that sick asshole to death outside. One swing. I gave myself one fucking punch. Any more violence, I'd go to jail for murder, and I can't stand the thought of leaving Ara forever. Or Erin and Beetle.

But in my mind, as that piece of shit fell to the ground, I ripped his jaw off. Peeled his skin away. Gouged out his eyes and cut off his dick. Set him on fire and pissed on the ashes. Even now, I can't seem to calm the fuck down. I should have followed through with my impulses. Fuck the consequences.

It was bad enough Jason made Ara feel like shit about herself. It was doubly bad that he kept boomeranging back to beg her to be with him. But that he violated her privacy, recorded her like that without her consent… and put a tracking program on her laptop, too. I can't believe how much danger she's been in and didn't know it.

And those pictures. I couldn't even look past the first thumbnail in that secret folder. Jason was a twisted son of a bitch who deserves everything he's going to get.

I should have killed him.

Now there's too much anger in me. Too much disgust. I'm pissed at myself for holding back.

Why do I always hold back?

I held back tonight when I should have unleashed unholy fury on that sick fuck.

I held back months ago when I should have asked Ara out. Then that shithead would have never existed in her life.

I held back when I was a kid, and never spoke my feelings or said what was on my mind.

I always hold back.

Not anymore.

I grab Ara by her ass, kneading her backside as I carry her into my bedroom. She's frantic and sad and I'm not letting her stay like this a minute longer. We've had a great few days and tonight was, in a twisted way, a good night too. We're about to put a very bad man behind bars.

"You did so good," I say against her mouth. She whimpers, rejecting my words. "You're so strong." She doesn't act like it now. "My girl is so brave and fierce." I lay her back on the bed. I'm not sure if she wants to be touched or not. She's in a shell.

I pivot my plan. "Come on."

I end up taking Ara back to her studio. This is her safe space. Her outlet. She needs this more than I need to claim her. As bad as I want to fuck her senseless and be a beast about it, a feral monster isn't what she needs tonight. She needs someone patient and understanding.

I hold her hand and guide her up the steps to her workspace. Digging her keys out for her, I unlock the door and flick on the lights.

Her demeanor shifts a little once she steps inside her art room. Ara lets out a little sigh and I know I've done the right thing bringing her here.

In silence, I tug her shirt over her head. Slip her feet out of her shoes and pull her pants off after that. Then I walk over and drag a small table with all her paint bins and jars of brushes over to the middle of the room. Without saying a word, I sit in the corner and watch what she does.

Ara doesn't look at me. Doesn't acknowledge my presence whatsoever. I'm okay with that.

She scrubs her face and stares at her feet. She's standing in the paint we fucked on earlier. Yanking her hair up, she redoes her messy bun, then grabs a canvas from the far side of the room. She props it so I can't see what's on it.

My girl plucks colors out of bins and loads her palate next.

Watching her work calms me. Settles my demons. Turns my scattered thoughts into actual reasonable sentences.

Ara works for hours in silence. My eyes grow heavy. I'm fucking exhausted, but I don't dare doze off. I keep watching her. She eventually grabs the bowl of Skittles and I hear her chew. She's hungry. I want to order food to be delivered, but I'm not risking breaking her spell. She's in a zone. I can feel it.

I love it.

I don't know how long I've been sitting here, but it must be going on twenty-four hours. I've already texted my manager to let him know I won't be in for a few days. My shop runs fine without me. Rubbing the heel of my palms against my eyes, I yawn. All my fight has left me. I'm just glad Ara's painting and her mood's shifted to a better one.

"Want to see it?" she croaks. Her voice is as tired as I feel.

I slowly get up and make my way to her. My body is killing me. I'm utterly exhausted. From my seat, all I got a view of was the back of a canvas and the table with all the paint and brushes scattered on it. I couldn't even see the top of Ara's head. But when I walk around it, I'm greeted with vibrant colors. It was so cold and empty on my side of the room, but Ara's is warm, energized. Brilliant.

Now I'm fully awake. "Holy shit."

She's painted me. It's the sketch from the other day of my face, but in full detail, with a fuckload of color added to it.

I can't stop staring at it. My face is broken into bits, like my facial cells are glitching. My throat has the word *Deep* blended into it. Computer code looks like it's pouring over my head, but there are words hidden in it. Some cut deep and are harsh. *Weak. Lost. Silent.* Others are nice. *Safe. Sublime. Strong.* The letters run into each other and drip down my head and face. Not like in the Matrix. No, this is more like thick green honey that spills over me, melting into different shades of rainbow colors on the bottom. *Family. Friend. Father figure.*

My eyes are fierce and confident in this painting. My jaw is clenched like it is now, and I automatically try to relax it.

There are more words hidden in my hair. *Grief. Grace. Generous.* The details are insane. It looks like a photograph, not a painting. How the fuck did she do this?

"I want to paint you more," she says. Her voice is strong. Eager. "I want to fill an entire art gallery with you."

I'm not sure what to say. I'm not sure where my voice is. I don't think I'm standing any more.

Ara's captured the essence of everything I've felt for over a decade. I feel seen. Vulnerable. I stare at my eyes and in the pupils are two very small words. *Ara* is in one. In the other is *Kitty*.

"It still needs a few—"

"It's perfect," I rush to say. "It's... I can't understand how you did this but it's..." My chest hurts. "This is incredible, Ara."

"It's raw and personal."

She's not wrong. "Why did you make your names so small in my eyes?"

"You noticed those?" She laughs, and I swear I finally feel my stress pop free from my body. "I didn't want to overpower your features."

"You should scroll your name across my forehead."

"Well, there's an idea."

"Exactly." Because she's my only thought. All my brain latches onto. "Can we take it home?"

"Home?"

"Yeah." I cock my eyebrow at her. "Home." Because Ara's coming home with me and that's where she'll live until she says otherwise. "If you hate my house, I'll buy us a different one."

"Slow down, big guy."

"Nope." I get all up in her space. "No more slowing down. No more holding back."

"The paint has to dry."

"Is that a yes? You'll move in with me?"

"I'll have to break my lease."

"That's okay. I'll cover it."

"We have to split the bills."

The fuck we do. "We'll negotiate that later." She's not paying a dime for our living situation.

"Are we really doing this?"

"Are you saying yes, Kitty?"

She beams me a smile, and I'm on cloud nine when she says, "Yes."

I kiss her, and this time I don't hold back. Neither does she.

Ara's mine now, tomorrow, forever.

EPILOGUE

Ara

"Fuck… me… harder… *harder*!" I hold on for dear life as Glitch rails me in the back room of his shop. The Computer Cave doesn't open for another three hours, giving us plenty of time to set up.

This past year has been a whirlwind of excitement.

I moved in with Glitch the night he asked. Three months later, he surprised me with a house that has a small building out back that's my new amazing art studio. The ribbon cutting ceremony for one of the murals I painted — in Beetle's elementary school, by the way — made headlines in the local paper, which caught the attention of some big wigs, and I've been working on steady commission pieces ever since.

I also have gallery space. Yup. You heard me right. Turns out Carson wasn't such a huge dick after all. He only ever acted obnoxious to get a rise out of Glitch, so he'd open up and talk to me. Dipshit thought pissing Glitch off would mean he'd stick up for me or say something to shut Carson up on my behalf. Apparently, me always trash talking back was *not* in Carson's plan. And the guy is connected as fuck. He asked one night while we were all playing Titan Fall if I wanted him to pass my portfolio around. I said yes—because I'm all about expanding my opportunities and getting my art out there—and now I've got my own space.

It's insane.

"Gonna fill you with my cum, Kitty." Glitch is in rare form this morning. I made him watch me get off in the shower without participating. Then I made him watch me play with my lipstick vibrator while he drove us to the Computer Cave. It took him five seconds to unlock the door, punch the security code, and carry me back here to fuck me.

He roars with his climax and pours himself into my body.

"Can't believe you made me wait to get inside to fuck you, Ara."

I laugh. "That's payback."

Last week, Glitch made me wear a bullet for a day and he had the power to control the settings with his phone. I nearly passed out in the middle of my morning walk. Then I fell on my knees in the grocery store, right in the frozen food aisle. I could have killed him. Would have had I not been completely blissed out by the time he made it home from work.

He's always experimenting with new tricks and toys. My man is a dirty mouthed, sexy, smart unicorn demon and I'm so damn happy he's mine.

"Glitch," I groan when he goes down on me. My body is hypersensitive all the time. He keeps my fires lit and never says no to me. I'm pretty sure he's a sex god sent to wreak havoc on my soul. "Oh my fuuuuck." My thighs clamp down around his ears as I come.

"Again." His growl and big dick make me wild. I come so fast a second time, it's hardly fair. "Too quick, Kitty. Again." He makes me hold out this time. Makes the sensations build until I'm begging for release.

Did I mention I suspect he's a sex god? I think so, but… my head's so fucking fuzzy right now.

He pulls out and I slide to my knees, taking him in my mouth to suck him off while I rub my clit. We come at the same time. We're getting great at the timing. I use my teeth and scrape them up his length before licking the rim of his dick and lapping up all his pleasure so I don't waste a drop.

"You're going to kill me one day, I swear it."

He might be right. "You'll die happy, so don't worry about it."

Glitch grabs me by the back of my head and kisses me so hard he steals my breath. We're getting married in a month. He's been hellbent on putting a baby in me. I'm excited at the idea of having a little Glitchy Ara running around, but I don't mind if it takes a while to get pregnant. I'm having too much fun being us right now. If it happens, great. If not, also great. Besides, Beetle keeps us busy. For now, we're practicing and having fun.

"I can't believe you talked me into this," I say, out of breath. Grabbing my shorts from the floor, I slip them back on and wobble.

"You love it. Don't lie."

"I didn't say I didn't love it. I just can't believe you talked me into it."

"You being Beetle's aunt is like his biggest flex." Glitch buttons his shirt and runs a hand through his hair. He has bright paint splotches tattooed on his inner thigh that are still healing.

"I'm not a flex."

"Yeah, you are." He slaps my ass. "And he's proud of you. Let him show his friends how cool you are."

"Ugh." I bite my lip and fix my hair. "What if they think it's losery?"

"Is that even a word?"

"It is now."

"It's not losery. Honestly, I think it's great. One more way to give back to the community, right?"

Speaking of that. I donated half my commission from the elementary school project to the local Grief Center that helps families who've lost loved ones. Erin said it helped her and Glitch when their parents died, so I wanted to show support however I could. Glitch, unbeknownst to Erin, has been donating to them since he graduated high school.

I want to donate to a sexual abuse charity next.

Jason's in jail, by the way, and will be for a long time. *Good fucking riddance.*

I'm making a list of all the organizations I want to donate to, because it's nice to give back to the community. It's even better than I'm starting to earn enough money to do it. Which brings me to these art classes I'm teaching at the Computer Cave.

They're free to whoever wants to take them. I plan to come in twice a week for two hours after school lets out during the school year. We haven't figured out a summer schedule yet. Maybe I'll put together an art camp or something.

"What if they don't want to draw anime?"

Glitch lifts his eyebrow. "You're testing me, Kitty."

I also fucked with all the dishes in the dishwasher last night. He'll spank me when he discovers the bowls on are on the bottom rack and all his precious forks are... *wait for it...* tines down.

I can't wait.

Glitch heads to the main part of the shop and starts scooting tables together. I'm worried.

What if this idea flops? Kids are judgy as shit and mean. I swear I don't know how my mother loved being a teacher. Kids can be tough.

What if Beetle is disappointed? What if he invites all his friends and they don't show? He's only just stopped being bullied. What if it starts it back up?

I grab Glitch's waist—a silent signal that lets him know I need reassurance.

He cups my chin. "You've got this."

But do I?

Two hours later, he opens the door and an hour after that, Beetle comes in. He drops his bookbag on the floor against the wall and runs to the chair he prefers.

Two more kids come in shortly after. Then another four.

Six.

Two more after that.

Fifteen kids total show up for the first lesson.

"Soccer lets out soon," a girl says. "I think the team's all coming. That's what my mom told me."

I gawk at Glitch. "We need more chairs."

"I'm on it." He gets busy and before I can grasp the situation, the Computer Cave is crammed with kids of varying grade levels. Many know Glitch already, but none of them have met me yet.

"Gentleman, this is Ara. Treat her with respect or you're out."

They don't even try to make a joke about it. Then again, Glitch has a reputation for teaching kids how to show respect.

I blow out a big breath and glance at Glitch, who's standing by the counter. He winks, and I roll my shoulders back. "Soooo, let's get started."

It's the most fun two hours in a room packed with kids I've ever had.

When it's over and the last kid leaves, I feel so alive, I'm vibrating. "That was fun and exhausting."

Glitch kisses the side of my neck. "You did amazing."

Every day we'll pull a character name out of a box, and I'll teach them how to draw it. Then I'll go over the basics of self-portraits, color balance, and the use of negative space. This first lesson was simple and fun and I'm so happy they enjoyed it.

"It gets easier." Glitch folds up the extra chairs and puts them away. "When I first started letting kids come here after school, it was mayhem. I panic bought a bunch of board games because I didn't have consoles for everyone to be on an Xbox at the same time and shit. So I busied them with other activities, got them into different conversations. They started treating this place like a second home. Talked around the tables while they played together. Did their homework and helped each other study."

I'd noticed they put all their trash away and pushed their chairs in before they left too. Glitch is a great role model.

I gather my art supplies. "Did you see their faces tonight when they held up their artwork to show each other?"

"Yeah, I did. They were proud of themselves. You gave them confidence, Ara. That's no small feat."

Art does that. Glitch does too.

"I love you," I say, dragging him in for a kiss.

He bites my lip playfully. "Thank you, Kitty. You've made me the happiest motherfucker on the planet."

"Just the planet?"

"Galaxy."

"Too late. You blew it."

"Universe."

"Too late!" I smack his arm.

He grabs my hand and kisses my knuckles. My big ass engagement ring could chip his tooth. "How do I ever make it up to you?"

I glance down at his hard-on. He's unbelievably insatiable… just like me. "I'm pretty sure my imagination can conjure up an idea or two." Or ten.

"You do have a very dirty mind."

"And you have one hell of a dirty mouth."

"Speaking of which…" Glitch hands me a pair of Bluetooth cat ear headphones. "I have a new one for you to listen to while we drive home." He places them over my ears and winks before pulling his phone out and hitting play.

My pussy swells the instant I hear his deep, dirty voice growl in my ear. *"Heyyyyy, Kitty."*

OTHER BOOKS BY THIS AUTHOR

Hell Hounds Harem Series:
Restless Spirit
The Dark Truth
The Devil's Darling
Hard To Find
Hard To Love
Hard To Kill
Raise Hell
Raise the Dead
Ruler of the Righteous

Sins of the Sidhe Series:
Shatter
Shine
Passion
Bargains
Ignite
Awaken
Rise
Exile
Discord

The Reflection Series:
Burn for Her
Lured by Her
Struck by Her

For information on this book and other future releases, please visit my website: www.BrianaMichaels.com

If you liked this book, please help spread the word by leaving a review on the site you purchased your copy, or on a reader site such as Goodreads.

I'd love to hear from readers too, so feel free to send me an email at: sinsofthesidhe@gmail.com or visit me on Facebook: www.facebook.com/BrianaMichaelsAuthor

ABOUT THE AUTHOR

Briana Michaels grew up and still lives on the East Coast. When taking a break from the crazy adventures in her head, she enjoys running around with her two children. If there is time to spare, she loves to read, cook, hike in the woods, and sit outside by a roaring fire. She does all of this with the love and support of her amazing husband who always has her back, encouraging her to go for her dreams.

Printed in Great Britain
by Amazon